GILA!

KATHRYN PTACEK
WRITING AS LES SIMONS

There was a moment of silence as the wind lulled, then a bloodcurdling scream. The kids pulled apart and stared around, their eyes large. The wind renewed its shrieking and howling. The boy's lower lip trembled, and he looked toward the waitress.

Reflexively, Erlinda pulled out the 12-gauge shotgun from behind the counter. She'd kept it there ever since that crazy guy with the .45 had come crashing into the diner late one night years before, demanding all the money, telling her to lie down on the floor so that he could use her. She'd been lucky that night. A sheriff's deputy had just gone off-duty and was eating there, and had shot the guy in the chest before anyone was hurt. Tomás had bought her the shotgun the next day, and it was never far away.

She checked the barrels. Both were loaded.

Licking her lips, Erlinda slowly advanced toward the diner's door.

The teenagers had scrambled up from their booth and were backing toward the counter, their hands gripped in fright.

Red Chief never looked up. He just kept sleeping and snoring.

Hiss. Hiss.

The sound was loud, louder than the wind.

Something was on the other side of the door.

Erlinda's heart hammered in her chest, and her palms were sweaty. She couldn't get frightened; it would freeze her up. She would put a bead on whoever—whatever—it was….

Erlinda raised the shotgun to her shoulder, sighted, and began to squeeze the trigger.

With a resounding crash that shook the entire diner, the door and wall caved in, the plaster dust rising in great clouds.

Forgotten, the shotgun dropped, and Erlinda screamed and screamed and screamed.

Author's Foreword to the 2012 Edition

Given that the world of publishing can be somewhat wacky, topsy-turvy, and utterly perplexing, *Gila!* was the third novel I sold, but was the very first one to show up in print. The book was penned by "Les Simons"—my dad's name was Lester, but he was called Les, so this was a tip of my writer's hat to him, and, well, Simons was nice and s-s-sibilant.

NAL released the novel about a million years ago (the early '80s) at a time when the folks at New American Library were publishing what we all called "big bug books," even though the critters weren't all bugs or huge. But they were out of control—nature gone amok! Leeches. Slugs. Bats. Crabs. I had visited editorial offices in New York City with my then-agent, filled up on all those books flung my way, and when I started reading them, I thought, hey, I can write one of these! It would be fun!

And the very first thing I thought about as my "big bug" was Gila monsters—giant Gila monsters, of course, because I lived in New Mexico, and all those intriguing yet cheesy movies of the '50s and early '60s had overly-large critters in them ... all mutated by ... EVERYONE SAY IT TOGETHER! ... radiation! And, yes, New Mexico was home to the Trinity Site, where the first atomic bomb was tested. How could I not connect the two?

There was also the apocryphal story told by my parents of their visit to the Trinity Site while my mother was pregnant with me.

i

They lived in Southern New Mexico at the time, and being rock hounds, they were out on a collecting trip; my mother tumbled out of the car and was heading toward the fence surrounding the test site when my dad asked her what she was doing. "I want a rock for my collection," she replied. He suggested that she might not want a glow-in-the-dark rock. I don't know what her response was, but I'm guessing it was choice. True or not, it's a story that shaped me in some fashion, I'm sure. Well, that and the fact that my parents often claimed that Martians brought me to them. Hmm. So, of course, I was drawn to that location for my book.

Meanwhile, back to giant lizards. As it happens, when I was only four or five, I went to the Albuquerque Zoo with a kindergarten class ... we saw lots of animals, ate lots of junk food that probably made us sick, and the only thing I could talk about, and indeed, the only thing I remember from that excursion, was the Gila monster lounging on a large flat rock. I don't remember any cute fuzzy animals, nor funny monkeys (although I'm not a fan), nor zebras or any other exotic critter ... I just remember this incredibly striking black and orange lizard.

I was so excited when I received the galleys for *Gila!* Back then (in those prehistoric publishing days), the galleys were one long continuous roll of paper—I don't even remember how it was sent to me. I just remember unscrolling that long, long, long thing and thinking, how am I going to proof the galleys? Well, I managed, of course, but right away I noticed something weird. ALL of the Spanish names in my novel had been changed. And believe me, those were a lot of changes since this book was set in New Mexico, land of the three cultures: Indian, Anglo, and Spanish. I didn't even recognize these new names. But an acquaintance, who just happened to be half-Puerto Rican, took a look at the names and declared them to be Puerto Rican names! In a book set in New Mexico. Apparently, the typesetters or copyeditors didn't get out of

New York City much and were thus unacquainted with the different Spanish names.

I wrote a note to the NAL copywriter and said that the names had to be stetted, and then I proceeded to change all the names back to the way I'd written them. This meant I had to consult my copy of the manuscript, and this was a very time-consuming task, since this was all done by hand, it being the days before computers. Yes, *Gila!* was typed on an electric typewriter. In fact, my first four novels were typed that way. Do I miss typewriters? Only the sound of the keys! This whole incident proved a good lesson. I was a novice writer and had thought publishers were infallible—I was wrong about that, and afterward, I was very obsessive with galleys and always checked them carefully word for word.

Not long after *Gila!* hit the stands in October of '81, I returned to Albuquerque to visit friends and family, and I also had a book signing lined up at a local bookstore. My friend, writer Bob Vardeman, showed up for moral support. The only other person in the store was an eleven- or twelve-year-old kid, who picked up a copy of the book, studied the semi-lurid cover, and announced, "That looks more like a Mexican beaded lizard." At this point, Bob and I just laughed … who the heck knows about those? Well, I did, of course, from having done research on these two poisonous lizards! And I don't even remember if the kid bought a copy or not. I hope he did!

My favorite memory of *Gila!*, though, is of the night I arrived at Newark Airport. I was flying to New Jersey to start a new life. Meeting me there was Charlie Grant, whom I would marry in a few months. He stood at the far end of the long concourse that all deplaning passengers had to walk through, and he was practically jumping up and down as he held aloft a book. And yeah, he was nearly waving the paperback. It was a copy of *Gila!*, which he had found in the airport bookshop and promptly purchased. I'm not sure who was more thrilled right then—Charlie or me—but it's a moment I won't ever forget ... seeing him with that book and that big grin on his face.

I hope you have a big grin on your face when you read *Gila!* Or at least put your tongue in your cheek as I did when I wrote the novel ... Enjoy this brief peek into New Mexico's sun and sand and giant deadly lizards. *Hiss.*

Kathryn Ptacek
Newton, NJ
January 2012

Prologue

… And the green lizards, and the golden snake,
Like unimprisoned flames, out of their trance awake.

SHELLEY, *Adonais*

The cloud welled up, expanding, towering, looming, blossoming. Up, up, up into the shape of a mushroom. The wind surged, screaming and sweeping outward in a circle of total destruction. Plants withered, animals died, stone and sand melted and fused.

The wind of destruction and change spread.

Then, abruptly, the destruction lessened, decreased. The radiation had already seeped, changing what it touched.

And on the fringes of that wide circle, the lizards watched.

Chapter 1

Erlinda Gonzales glanced up at the clock as she washed the grease off the red countertop. Eleven thirty-five. Twenty-five minutes more, and the El Ranchito Carry-out Diner/Reptile Gardens/Curio Shop on the highway turnoff to the White Sands National Monument would close for the night, and then she could leave.

As she pushed back a strand of black hair, the Chicana sighed, for it had been a long, exhausting day. It had been hot, unusually so for mid-September, and the air was sluggish. The metal fan, set high on a shelf, merely served to push hot air from one end of the small diner to the other. The Ranchito had no air-conditioning. Maybe, if she opened the windows, she'd catch a cool night breeze. The stocky woman glanced at the red curtains. No, there'd be dust all over by morning.

Wearily she recalled the day's cranky turistas, who'd complained continually about everything. And there'd been wrong orders and broken crockery, as well; and Tiny, the cook, had been in a foul mood since midmorning when he'd burned his hand on the grill.

And she was uneasy; she didn't know why. Perhaps it was the heat of the day. Maybe it would rain.

Sometimes she felt uncomfortable before a change of weather. The wind blew now, a low moaning sound that put her teeth on edge.

2

Still, soon, so very soon she would be going home, and Tomás would be waiting in bed for her. And she would slip into his arms, and the uneasiness and tiredness would disappear, and things would become much, much better. Yet home was a twenty-mile drive along a darkened road not much better than a washboard. At least the jolts would knock the dust of the day off. But the six-o'clock alarm would ring and the same tired routine would begin again. The same kinds of customers, the same kinds of problems, over and over.

With a jangle of India cow bells the door opened, a gust of wind sweeping in, and the woman glanced with resignation at the new customer, struggling to close the door.

It was Billy "Tex" Perkins, an old regular and independent trucker. He was friendly, chatty, and always left a good tip. The rangy man slid onto a brown-and-white cowhide bar stool at the counter.

"The same as usual, Erlinda," he said, then leaned back, cupping his hands, to light a cigarette. He inhaled quickly, the smoke streaming out of his nostrils in two pencil-thin lines.

She called over her shoulder to the cook in the kitchen. "Four over easy, stack of cakes." Wiping her hands on her yellow apron, she poured the man a cup of coffee. "How's business been? You're late tonight. I expected you over an hour ago." Erlinda pushed the cup across to him.

"Got delayed." Tex traced the wet ring left by the cup with a tobacco-stained finger. "Good goin's lately. Could be better, though." He shrugged. "Or worse." He grinned suddenly. "Whyn't you come along with me sometime, Erlinda?"

She studied the creases in his face, the wind-beaten and tanned skin, and smiled. For years he had been asking that of her. She wondered what would happen if she said yes someday. But it wasn't likely, not with dark-haired Tomás to go home to.

He drained his cup and held it out for more coffee.

"Comin' here tonight I seen this big animal just outside of my headlights. Really strange, y'know? Could have sworn it was a coyote. Maybe a wolf. Maybe just a big tumbleweed."

She grinned. "Maybe it's a camel left over from the cavalry days."

The trucker laughed. "Could be." He lit another cigarette.

Above the groaning wind, a muffled giggle sounded from a secluded corner booth, back behind the now-silent jukebox, and Erlinda came around the corner. She crossed her arms and stared disapprovingly.

"Okay, you kids, break it up. You know the rules. Order or get out." Her voice was firm, yet her dark eyes were slightly amused.

The embracing couple pulled apart, and the blonde girl patted her bouffant hairdo. She tittered nervously, and twin spots of red appeared on her cheeks. The boy dropped his eyes to the table, then moved his hand surreptitiously as he closed his zipper. Erlinda sighed.

"Oh, we'll take two Cokes, please," the brown-haired boy said at last. He nervously played with a button on his shirt and refused to meet Erlinda's eyes. The girl beside him wiggled.

As Erlinda walked away, she could still hear their furtive whispers. "Hey, watch it, Steph, that hurts!"

She shook her head, then paused at the booth closest to the counter. Red Chief, a fixture at the diner, slept with his old head cradled on the scarred plastic table. His green-and-black flannel shirt was threadbare in spots and one elbow poked out a ragged hole. His jeans were dusty, dirt caking the creases. The laces of his boots were long gone and the tongues flapped loosely when he walked.

Poor old man, she thought with pity. No one at home wanted him, not his son, his son's wife, nor their five children. His wife had been dead for twenty-three years. He didn't even have the dignity of his own revered ways, for Red Chief—Erlinda didn't even know

4

his real name—had worked for the white man all his life, had tried to live the way of the white man, and then in his old age, he had been rejected by the white man. In the past, the aged ones would have simply walked out into the desert until they dropped. Now, he slept in the diner, drinking away what little money he had, and wandered around the fringes of the desert, as if seeking an answer to his woes in nature.

The waitress got the drinks and eyed the kids as she set the glasses down with a sharp tap. "Your dad know where you are, Stephanie?" she asked the blonde.

The girl shrugged, a gesture made elaborately casual. "Oh, yeah."

Sure, Erlinda thought.

"You two gonna get in trouble one of these days," she said.

"Hey!" the boy, Steve, protested. He glanced at the girl, then at the woman. "We ain't doin' nothin' illegal. It could be worse; we could be neckin' out on the mesa."

"Yeah. But her father isn't goin' to stand for no boy messin' with his baby girl."

"I'm not a baby," the girl said loftily, and looked into the mirror of her compact. She tugged at her lacy white blouse and hastily buttoned one of the buttons that stretched across her full breasts.

"No. You're not," the woman admitted, deciding to leave them alone. As she rounded the counter, Tex leaned down to brush some dirt off his boots, then busily applied himself to his meal. She glanced back at the clock. Eleven forty-nine. Why did time pass so slowly at night? Especially before closing. She picked up the gray dishcloth and began wiping the counter surface again.

The wind rose in a steady howl, whistling through the crack around the windows and door. Sand shifted across the floor. *Damned white stuff*, the woman thought. Got in her hair, her clothes, all over the counter. Why the turistas were so eager to see a big sand box, she didn't know.

A prickling crept along her neck, tickling the back hair. On moonlit nights when the desert became a sea of white, as it was this night, the *abuelos* danced in the graveyards, holding skeletal hands and moaning the names of those about to die. Or so her grandmother would say. *Crazy old woman*, Erlinda thought, shrugging, dismissing her relative's mystical turn of mind.

"Them new boots?" she asked Tex with a vague nod of her head.

"Yeah." The trucker drew his legs up to better show off the black boots with the pointed toes and high heels. "Brand new. Paid two fifty for 'em," he said with a touch of pride in his voice.

"I think you got taken, Tex."

"Nah," he said, as he stirred his fork through his eggs. "They're genuine lizard skin."

"Yeah?" she asked with curiosity, and leaned across the counter. If she talked, she wouldn't notice the uneasy feelings. Unconsciously, she fingered the gold crucifix on a chain at the base of her throat. "What kind of lizard?"

"Dunno. Guess maybe it's just plain lizard lizard."

Another giggle burst from the booth where the two teenagers sat. Erlinda glanced up sharply, reprimand on her lips, when a horn honked outside. Another trucker? Should know that they didn't have outside waitress service.

The honking continued, the whining sound piercing the woman's head, even over the sound of the shrieking wind. "Sounds like your horn got stuck."

"Damn," the man said. He sipped his coffee and wavered, torn between finishing his meal and fixing the horn. It was obvious he didn't relish going back out into the sandstorm.

"Hey!" said the boy, looking at the trucker. Stephanie was frowning, the corners of her generous mouth mulishly pulled down. "Turn it off, man."

A new sound was added—that of metal being crushed or twisted.

"Goddamn, that tears it," Tex shouted, wiping his mouth and tossing down his paper napkin. "Some s.o.b.'s gone and hit my rig!" He stood up and in five strides had crossed the dirty expanse of the diner's floor. He slammed the door behind him so hard that the glass panes wobbled.

There was a moment of silence as the wind lulled, then a bloodcurdling scream. The kids pulled apart and stared around, their eyes large. The wind renewed its shrieking and howling. The boy's lower lip trembled, and he looked toward the waitress.

Reflexively, Erlinda pulled out the 12-gauge shotgun from behind the counter. She'd kept it there ever since that crazy guy with the .45 had come crashing into the diner late one night years before, demanding all the money, telling her to lie down on the floor so that he could use her. She'd been lucky that night. A sheriff's deputy had just gone off-duty and was eating there, and had shot the guy in the chest before anyone was hurt. Tomás had bought her the shotgun the next day, and it was never far away.

She checked the barrels. Both were loaded.

Licking her lips, Erlinda slowly advanced toward the diner's door.

The teenagers had scrambled up from their booth and were backing toward the counter, their hands gripped in fright.

Red Chief never looked up. He just kept sleeping and snoring.

Hiss. Hiss.

The sound was loud, louder than the wind.

Something was on the other side of the door.

Erlinda's heart hammered in her chest, and her palms were sweaty. She couldn't get frightened; it would freeze her up. She would put a bead on whoever—whatever—it was....

Erlinda raised the shotgun to her shoulder, sighted, and began to squeeze the trigger.

With a resounding crash that shook the entire diner, the door and wall caved in, the plaster dust rising in great clouds.

Forgotten, the shotgun dropped, and Erlinda screamed and screamed and screamed.

Chapter 2

Night falls quickly over the New Mexico desert, and with it comes a stillness. Thus, any sound is magnified far beyond its normal range.

And so it was on this September night, for although the noise was miles away, it could be distinctly heard, and the sound of it drove the night creatures deep into their burrows.

Down the road, the barely paved road that crept this way and that over the landscape, the sound came, growing louder and louder. Shrieking and yelling and laughing and singing. And with it could be heard a racing engine and rubber tires on tar surface.

The twenty-eight high school kids shouted and chanted.

"Las Quintas is *numero uno!*"

"*Numero uno!*"

"*Uno! Uno!*"

"Who is?"

"We are!"

"*Numero uno!*"

"*Uno!*"

The chant pounded into the driver's temples, and she momentarily touched a hand to her head, as if seeking to keep the noise out. Of course, it was futile. It always was. And it was somehow worse when she was driving the kids. If she could get an office job, away from the kids, the stupid buses … but none of them paid as well as this. And she needed the money, especially now that Dick had left her with the baby. Babies were expensive.

The kids were always noisy, but tonight was worse than usual, and the heat, the oppressive heaviness to the usually cool desert night air, only increased her discomfort.

The headlights swept arcs of light before the bus, briefly illuminating the mesquite and cacti along the sides of the road.

The driver, hunching forward, glanced up out of the windshield at the sky above. Abyss-black, as it can be only in the desert, far from the haze of city lights. The moon, with its pocked yellow face, was circled by a band of gray. Across the moon's face dark clouds scudded, growing ever thicker.

There was another burst of laughing and cheering, and the driver brought her thoughts back to the road and to the boisterous teenagers.

The Las Quintas High School had won the homecoming game against its fierce rival, El Yermo, and the teenagers were minutely reliving each moment. In the last two minutes of the game, the home team had recovered the ball. The score was 30-36. Grabbing the football, Ted "Paco" Smith had run forty yards for a touchdown, his white-clad legs blurring. With Paco's touchdown, the score was tied, and the fans in the old wooden bleachers went crazy. Streamers of toilet paper were tossed onto the field, firecrackers in the stands went off, and ice from soft drinks somehow found its way down the necks of fellow fans. Chants of "Paco, Paco, Paco" filled the night air. Then, with thirty seconds left in the fourth quarter, the school's prize kicker, a shy boy from a family of thirteen, had knocked the pigskin solidly between the goalposts. The buzzer soon went off, signaling the end of the game, and Las Quintas had won, 37-36.

Of course, the team couldn't just leave immediately after the ballgame. Cordelia Jenkins had paced alongside her yellow bus and smoked cigarette after cigarette, grinding the butt of each into the ground with her boots. The area of the bus seemed to be paved with filter tips by the time the kids showed up. It wasn't the kids' fault that they were delayed, that she would be driving these tortuous back roads at midnight when she was tired. Really, it wasn't. The little bastards. Didn't they realize she'd have to get up in the morning and get to work? She couldn't loll around the house, basking in their damned football glory. She had a baby to support after that goddamned …

But here they were.

The tired players straggled toward the bus, with the cheerleaders and coaching staff and well-wishers crowding behind them.

And now every glorious second had to be dissected and carefully examined.

"In the second quarter, man—"

"No, no, Willie, I mean when he took that long shot down the—"

"Man, is my mother gonna kill me. Look at these grass stains! They're never gonna get clean!"

"Who cares?"

"Did you see ol' Red's face when Paco ran with that ball?"

"I knew we had it in the first half!"

"Shee-et, man, we done good."

There was clapping and cheering and singing and whistling and stomping of feet, and among some of the boys in the back of the darkened bus, its windows opened to catch some little breeze in the stifling heat of the night, a bottle of cheap red wine was passed from player to player. Managers and coaches, sitting at the front of the bus, minded their own business; after all, it was dark. No one would be the wiser.

"Hey, Anita, come back here," one of the boys yelled to a pretty brunette sitting midway in the bus with six other girls. She turned her head and peered into the dark.

"Not on your life!"

"Aw, come on."

"No." But Anita smiled.

"For just a moment, *por favor*. I gotta surprise for you," the boy called, an appealing tone in his youthful voice.

The other girls tittered, and Anita waved her hand at them to quiet them. Standing, the head cheerleader tugged at the short white-and-maroon skirt. It barely covered the roundness of her firm bottom, and only accentuated her long strong legs.

Keeping a firm grip on the metal bars along the tops of the brown-leather seats, she swayed slowly down the aisle. The girl stared at the blond boy lounging on the long backseat. He was still in his maroon-and-white uniform with the numeral "10" in shimmering silver, and it hid little of the power in his muscular body.

"Yeah, Paco?"

The bus gave a sudden lurch as the driver swerved to avoid a pothole, and the girl, a surprised expression on her dark face, fell into the boy's lap.

"Now, that's just what I wanted," he said, grinning wolfishly.

"When is that all you've wanted?" Anita countered, trying to get up off his lap. His arms tightened around her.

"Just a kiss, Anita. One single kiss for the hero of our illustrious football team." His square hand moved along the silkiness of her leg to her short skirt. She slapped his hand.

"Get away, buddy."

"Anita." His voice took on a pleading tone.

"No, Paco."

The boy caressed her knee and his arms tightened around her, puffing her close to him. One hand touched the smoothness of her bottom, and it tugged at the elastic top of her maroon panties.

"Paco."

"Yeah?"

"Umm, Paco."

The two moved quietly on the backseat of the bus, oblivious to anyone else who might be watching or listening.

Christ, the driver thought as the first fat drops of rain hit the windshield. Switching on the wipers, she peered through the darkness. They *would* have to get caught in a cloudburst on their way home. All they needed now, God forbid, was a flat tire. Damned New Mexico weather. It could be clear one moment and raining the next—or even clear overhead *while* it was raining.

She wasn't looking forward to the stretch of road ahead. It narrowed to a lane barely wide enough for a midsized car. Damn burro trails in this state. The bridge over the Arroyo Peligroso was just two narrow lanes, and now there was this damned pelting rain. *A regular cloudburst*, she thought.

Cordelia peered again through the windshield. So much damned water made it hard to see.

She was so tired, so weary, and she longed for a cigarette. But not while she was driving. It was too difficult to take even one hand off the wheel on this road, particularly in these conditions.

No doubt that ass Dick was kicking up his heels with one of his numerous "lady friends." He'd certainly had enough when they were married. He didn't have to work all day and night to support an infant.

Those goddamned kids were so fucking noisy. The shouting and screaming pounded into Cordy's head, beating a staccato rhythm that threatened to explode her ears and the top of her head.

She whipped her head around, glaring at the kids. "Shut up, you fuckers," she shouted.

But it did no good. No one heard over the din of victory.

She faced the highway again and hunched her shoulders, then froze. Yellow flickered ahead. What was it?

Headlights? A car coming at them. Probably in the wrong lane. That's how they all drove on these back roads. *Jesus*, Cordelia thought, licking her dry lips. She peered through the gloom, then switched her own lights on bright.

Immense yellow eyes blinked at her. Over the noise of the teenagers and the pounding of the rain on the metal roof of the bus, she heard a hissing noise, like the sound of air escaping a tire.

Cordelia screamed. She jerked the wheel to the left to avoid hitting the thing in front of her.

The kids were thrown from the seats. Paco flew out of the backseat, halfway down the aisle. The shy kicker who'd nudged the score one point over the tie, hit a window with the side of his head, and the glass cracked, the breaks radiating like a spider's web. Anita fell off the seat onto the floor, caught in the tangle of her clothes.

But the bus was already speeding over the narrow bridge spanning the Arroyo Peligroso, swollen with flash-flood water. On the wet pavement, the yellow school bus swerved, sliding, and spun toward the bridge sides. Desperately Cordelia tried to regain control. It was useless.

Into the bridge's sidebars the vehicle crashed. Across empty air the bus flew. Then the law of gravity took hold. Down it arched, the screams of the teenagers inside blending with the hissing of the giant creature that fell with the bus.

The vehicle hit the sandy bottom of the arroyo, and the gas tank exploded. Flames, yards high, shot into the blackness of the New Mexico sky. The gasoline spread along the water, until it seemed the entire arroyo was on fire.

Inside, the screams grew fewer and fewer.

In a few minutes nothing could be heard but the padding of the rain, the crackling of the flames, and the sound of something large, something hissing, that slowly moved away from the scene.

Chapter 3

Dr. Kate Dwyer pushed back a strand of long red hair and stared down at the poisonous *Trimorphodon lambda* as it oozed along the bottom of its terrarium. The Sonora lyre snake's tongue flickered out briefly. The little brown mouse squeaked, tearing across the glass container and scrabbled panic-stricken at the glass sides.

As the snake captured its meal, Dr. Dwyer walked away from the table, sat at the desk, and began writing. She did not look up when a telephone rang in the next room. The sounds of reptiles slowly moving in their cages surrounded her in her laboratory. Sunlight glinted through the venetian-blind-shuttered windows, striping some of the tanks and cages.

The insistent ringing finally penetrated the woman's consciousness. She rose, frowning, and had crossed the lab when the sound stopped.

Exasperated, Kate turned to return to her desk, then walked across to the windows and raised one of the blinds. She gazed out at the campus of the University of New Mexico in Albuquerque.

The sunlight glinted on the adobe-style buildings. Everywhere she looked she saw pavement and dirt lots. In the distance she heard the faint sound of a lawn mower, and the sound reminded her of lazy summer days in the East. *But there,* she thought with a faint smile, *they had grass;* they had greenery and trees and water.

Here we have the Duck Pond, Kate reflected. *And Fort Ortega.* She remembered coming to the campus the first day and telling her department head that the building only lacked turret guns on the corners of the second floor. He hadn't appreciated her humorous suggestion.

To the east rose the Sandia Mountains and slightly above them was the sun. Thin clouds were scattered in the gold and coral sky. In the distance she saw a hot air balloon floating across the vista of the Sandias.

She sat down and was once more writing when the unoiled door squealed open, and Charlie Garcia stuck his head in.

"Phone for you in my office, Kate," he called.

"Um ... could you take a message for me, Charlie?" she asked, not looking up from the note pad. "I'm in the middle of something here."

"Don't think so."

She glanced up at the man's dark face. "Why not?"

"It's the governor's office calling."

"Governor?" Surprise crossed her pretty features. Her dark brows knitted with a brief frown. She left the lab. In the room across the hall she sat in an old leather chair and picked up the phone receiver. Unabashedly curious, Garcia lounged in the doorway.

"Hello? ... Yes, it is.... The governor? Today?" Kate paused to look at Garcia, who smiled. "Well, I have a class at one. Yes ... I can get someone else to handle it. Sure ... I understand. My car's in the garage, though." She paused again, listening. "Government plane? All right. I'll be up there in about an hour. Fine. I'll see you then."

She quietly hung up the receiver, then stared through the window for a few moments.

"Charlie?"

"Yeah?"

"You doing anything at one?"

"I think," he responded slowly, "that I'm about to acquire another class."

She faced him with a faint frown. "Do you mind taking it?"

"No. Just as long as you tell me what the governor's office wanted." He grinned at her and cocked an eyebrow.

"That's easy enough," the woman said. "They wouldn't tell me. It's a big fat surprise."

"Well," Garcia said, "I'll take you to the airport and then we can try to figure out this puzzle. Maybe he wants to ask you about a snakeskin band for his Stetson!"

"Charlie!" But Kate laughed. "C'mon. Let's go."

"Miz Dwah'yer, it's a real plea-shure to meet y'all." The big burly governor of New Mexico oozed from behind his walnut desk to shake her offered hand.

Irritably she found herself wishing she could stick him with a cattle prod so that the man would talk a little faster. He was dressed in a flat brown western shirt and pants, western boots, and had on a bolo tie, the silver clasp of which was shaped like a steer's head. Its eyes were turquoise nuggets.

"It's a pleasure, Governor Roy," Kate said dryly, then paused. "And it's *Dr.* Dwyer."

"Why, that's right." He smiled. "Ah'm right sorry 'bout that, Doctor. Dwah'yer."

She smiled. Faintly.

"Y'all kin call me Bubba." He grinned.

"Yes, thank you, Governor."

He went on, unaware of the irony in her words. "Now, Ah need y'all to examine somethin' fer me. Ah'm well aware of y'all's reppytation as a herpe"—he paused, tried again—"herpo, er, hippotoligist."

"Herpetologist," she corrected.

"Why, thank y'all, ma'am." Bubba Roy continued. "And ah thought of y'all immediately, 'specially after readin' that article 'bout y'all in the na-yoospahper. Now, whyn't y'all come with me?"

The governor beckoned with one meaty hand. Kate waited for him to leave the office. His shoulders were almost too broad to go through the doorway. His head seemed to sit on them, as if there were no neck. She remembered the campaign two years before — his body had been part of his campaign hysteria — "A solid man for a solid job."

Out of his office they walked, down a series of marble corridors in the state capitol building past curious civil servants who stared at her, rather than at him. She was aware how they must look to observers. A tall, well-built woman with red hair, striding down the hall with this stubby clown of a politician. *Very amusing*, she thought. They came to a staircase with worn steps. Reaching the basement, they moved along a dusty corridor, to what appeared to be a storeroom. As the governor entered, two guards snapped to attention.

What was going on? Kate asked herself. Why the secrecy? Especially in the basement of the Merry Round House?

Governor Roy went over to a white freezer, a model that opened from the top, and waved to the guards.

They lifted something large, wrapped in black plastic, and placed the object on a workbench. The governor gestured to Kate to move closer. She switched on an additional overhead light, and in the harsh glare of the unshaded bulb, unwrapped the plastic. She stared.

The object was large, about four feet in length, and appeared to be a fleshy cone tapering to a blunt tip at one end. The other was jagged, as though torn. The exterior appeared to be seared, making it impossible to identify the original color. She ran her hand across the object, feeling the scaly texture, and frowned. She dusted her hands, watching the ice slivers from the thing's stay in the freezer fly off.

"Wall?"

She glanced at the governor, at the two guards, all of whom were intently watching her. "I'd like to run some tests, if you don't mind, Governor." She glanced back at the object.

He waited.

Obviously it was just a part, she told herself; had once been alive; was almost certainly a reptile. But … No buts until she got to her lab, she told herself firmly.

"Wall?" Governor Bubba Roy asked again. "Doctor Dwah'yer, what is it?" His beady brown eyes bored into her.

She glanced up at him, her blue eyes serious. "The tip of a tail—from a lizard."

Chapter 4

"Where's Steph?" Brad Lewis asked, walking over to the white range and pouring himself a cup of coffee. The lanky man sat at the table, leaned back in the chair, and sipped at the steaming liquid. He glanced out the window. Still fairly dark — it would be a cloudy day. Maybe there would be more rain.

Corinne Lewis, a tanned woman who looked far older than her forty years, never looked up from the newspaper. She automatically reached for her cup, swallowed some coffee, and continued reading. "I don't know, Brad," she said after a while. "Haven't heard a peep from her. Maybe she left already."

Brad Lewis glanced up at the large-faced clock, set in a ceramic cactus, then back at his wife. "Going on six. Stephanie's never got up before nine in her life, if she could help it. Laziest thing I ever saw."

"Brad!" the blonde woman protested.

"It's true," the rancher said, finishing the cup of coffee. "It's time she was gettin' up, anyway. She's probably been out all night with that no-good—"

"Now," Corinne warned, "don't get all riled up about Steve."

Brad shrugged, poured another cup of coffee. He sipped at it for a few minutes more, then pushed back his chair with a scrape. Leaving the kitchen, he walked down the hail to the last door and knocked sharply.

"Stephanie," Brad called through the thick wooden door. "Get up!"

There was no answer.

"Get up, honey!" He rapped repeatedly.

Again no one answered.

Frowning, Brad put his hand on the doorknob and turned it. The door swung open and he entered his daughter's bedroom.

It always made him uncomfortable, this room, and the feeling returned as he stared at the dainty white furniture, the stuffed bears and cats and lambs scattered across the room, the snapshots of past boyfriends and movie stars stapled to the wall. The window was open, the screen removed, and the pink-and-white dotted-Swiss curtains were blowing straight back with the force of the morning breeze. He glanced around, saw the closet door half open, a pair of nylon panty hose trailing out of the recess.

"Stephanie?" he called again, even though it was now quite apparent she wasn't in the room. He left the bedroom, followed the hallway, and glanced in the kitchen.

Corinne was still reading. "Find her?" she asked absently.

"No," Brad said. "I'll check around outside."

Walking out of the ranch house, he crossed the dirt yard to the garage. The blue Chevy was there, the red Ford truck, the jeep, and the old sedan.

He frowned.

"Good morning, Señor Lewis," said a voice.

He looked up to see Manuel Martinez, one of his hired hands, coming into the garage. The Chicano took off his worn cap and shifted from foot to foot.

"Mornin', Mannie. You see Miss Stephanie this mornin'?"

"No, sir. I doan' see her since last night after dinner," the Chicano said apologetically.

"After dinner?" the rancher asked sharply.

"Yessir. She gone out with that boy." Manuel refrained from mentioning the boy's name.

"Goddammit," the rancher exploded.

"Yessir."

Brad whirled away from the garage, running across the yard. He slammed the screen door to the kitchen, and Corinne looked up, startled.

"Brad! What's the matter?" she called anxiously at his retreating back.

"Goddamn boy," he shot back as he ran into one of the rooms.

"What?"

He came out to the kitchen again, and in his hands was a deadly-looking weapon.

"Brad, no!" The woman was on her feet, trying to plant herself in front of him. "Brad, stop it!"

"I'm gonna kill that boy," he said in a low voice, a wild look in his eyes. "He's been messin' with my daughter, and I'm gonna blow his balls off."

"Brad!" Corinne screamed. "For God's sake, you can't—"

He turned to look at her. "I can, and I will."

With a slam of the door Brad was gone, and she heard the sounds of the Ford truck's engine turning over. Corinne Lewis rushed out into the yard, her sun-streaked blonde hair blowing in the breeze. But her husband was already pulling out of the garage, backing up past the pump, parallel to the fence.

With a squeal the gears shifted and the truck shot forward. She turned around, walked back into the house, and sat once more at the table, knowing that nothing would stop her husband until he found the boy. She thought of calling the sheriff, hesitated, then decided she should.

The pickup jounced along the unpaved road, but Brad Lewis, unseeing, saw nothing of the grama grass, the tumbleweed, the cacti.

He knew where those goddamned kids were, where they always were. Goddamned Mexican just let them hang out there all night long. God knows what she encouraged them to do.

The speedometer crept higher, passing fifty, fifty-five, sixty, and then seventy. The wind shrieked in at him from the open windows, and sand blew in, gritting in his eyes and his mouth, drying them out.

He wheeled the pickup down a fork, heading left, and he glanced in the rearview mirror, seeing the long dusty trail that marked the progress of his truck.

Ahead he spotted the sign for the El Ranchito Diner, sped past it, then slammed on the brakes.

"Holy shit," Brad said out loud, running a hand through his dusty hair.

He got out and looked around.

Twisted metal wreckage of what appeared to be a semi-tractor-trailer lay in front of the diner. The neon sign over the door was shattered; one entire wall was pushed in.

He cocked his shotgun and cautiously moved forward, wondering what had caused the wreckage.

None of the furniture inside was intact, and there were signs that the diner had been occupied when it was attacked. Overnight the desert scavengers had been busy. He pushed one of the bodies over with the toe of his boot.

It was Steve, the boy he'd come to kill, and both his hands were missing, as well as the front of his chest.

Bile rose in Brad's throat, threatening to choke him. Flies buzzed around a lump in the middle of the diner's floor, and he realized, looking at the long shiny black hair, that it had been Erlinda, the waitress.

He searched through the ruins, pushing boards to one side. He found two other bodies, both men, both defaced from the rodents. But there was no sign of Stephanie.

23

"Steph?" he called, hoping against hope that she might have lived through this carnage, that somehow she had gotten away. "Steph?" he repeated. "Where are you, hon?"

But no one answered Brad. He listened intently and all he heard was the sound of the wind and the moan of the sand as it crept across the ruins of the diner.

He walked out of the diner and looked around. Off to one side was a small lump. Brad walked quickly toward it. Long and flesh-toned. A girl's arm.

His heart hammered under his ribs. It couldn't be hers; no. It had to be someone else's. That boy had had to be out with someone else last night.

Brad started to turn away when something caught his eye. Horrified, unable to resist, he walked forward. It was round, and two sightless eyes stared up at him from his daughter's head. The right side was missing, as though something heavy and blunt had struck her, crushing the skull. Red and gray oozed out across the blonde hair onto the white sand.

The vomit rose in his throat and he was unable to contain it. On and on it poured, and there was no end to his nausea. He fell to his hands and knees, and the puddle before him increased. At last, his arms and legs trembling violently, he got slowly to his feet, his shotgun lying in the sand forgotten. He stumbled away from the half-eaten head of his daughter, past the ruined diner.

As he moved, strength came back to him, and he began running down the road to the phone booth. He pushed the door aside and fumbled with the receiver. Brad slipped two dimes into the slot and dialed with a shaking finger. He paused midway as he heard a slithering noise, then finished the phone number.

It rang and rang and rang.

God, let her be in, the rancher prayed silently. Let Corinne be there.

Another ring ... and another.

"Hello?"

"Corinne," he burst out. "My God, my God," he started to cry.

"Brad? What's wrong?"

The rancher, through his weeping, heard a low noise, like the sound of air escaping a car tire. He looked up.

"Brad!"

"Christ!" he screamed, and tried to get out of the phone booth, but the door jammed.

He shrieked, and the phone receiver dangled, with the small voice calling out to him, as the phone booth toppled backward and in an instant was crushed.

Chapter 5

"A lizard tail," Governor Bubba J. Roy repeated, yet Kate thought there was not much surprise in the man's voice.

"Yes," the woman responded. "It would have to be an extraordinarily large creature, of course, much like the Komodo dragon."

"Kimono dragon?" the governor asked, scratching his head.

"Komodo," Kate corrected. "It lives only on some small islands of Indonesia and can grow to a length of ten feet. It can tear off the hind legs of a boar and swallow bones and all."

He stared at her.

"We don't have anything that size in America," she said.

"Mebbe one of them Kimono draguns snuck over here," Governor Roy suggested seriously.

"I doubt it, Governor." She glanced back at the lizard tail. "Where was this found?"

"Wall, y'all seen the na-yoospahper this mornin'?" he asked unexpectedly.

"Yes." Kate frowned, wondering what this had to do with the lizard tail.

"Bout them poor kids on that school bus down to Otero County?"

"Yes."

26

Bubba J. Roy nodded with his chin, the sagging flesh underneath wobbling with the effort. "This here was found in the arroyo next to the bus. 'Course, the bus was all burned up, and this here tail was pretty well charred. We got two survivors, two kids thrown clear, down in the hospital in Alamogordo. Them kids are mighty shaken up, but it was rainin' heavy down there last night and they was comin' home from a football game, and they remember a little 'bout the accident. They keep mumblin' 'bout somethin' mighty large, and yellow eyes starin' in at them. This was just before the bus went over the side of the bridge."

"Were there any tracks?" the woman asked.

"Seemed to be, but they was washed out by all the rain." The governor looked at Kate. "Ah want y'all to go down there, Dr. Dwah'yer, and take a look around fer me."

"Me?" she asked with genuine surprise. "Why?"

"Y'all's a her-herpetologist, and this here is a lizard tail, and that seems to be y'all's department. Ah think it's mighty logical that y'all go down and see what y'all can find out."

"I'm flattered, of course, Governor Roy, that you should ask me, but shouldn't you be sending something like an investigating committee?" She glanced at the guards, but they were lounging now by the door, apparently unaware of this exchange.

"Miz Dwah'yer, Ah'll be frank with y'all. This here is an election year, and Ah'm up for reelection. In all honesty, Ah cain't send a government team 'cause of them gawddamned snoopy reporters that hang around the capitol. As it is, they're gonna be mighty interested in y'all's comin' here today. But it'd look a whole lot better fer y'all to go south and take a peek 'round. After all, y'all got the cree-dentials, and everybody knows university professors are a curious lot, always stickin' their noses into other's business. Jes' like reporters." The governor looked at her face and added hastily, "No offense meant, Doctor."

She looked at the charred tail, didn't bother to answer him. "When would you want me to go?" Kate asked.

"Right away, Doctor. Ah think the sooner we know what's goin' on down south, the better. We don't want no panic or nothin' terrible like that."

"From what you said—or didn't say—there's more to it than just the bus crash." Kate gazed at him shrewdly.

"That's right." He sighed deeply. "C'mon upstairs. Ah reckon we can leave this here tail down here now."

"I'll come back later, before I leave, and take a section," the biologist said.

The governor nodded to the two guards, who wrapped up the fleshy object, depositing it once more in the freezer. Kate followed the governor out of the basement room and up the stairs.

"Well, Governor Bubba J. Roy," came a dry, faintly sarcastic voice, "I found you at last. What are you doing lurking in the basement with such a lovely woman?" The voice now contained a polite leer.

Kate saw a tall man with brown hair, brown eyes, and a pale skin that looked faintly unhealthy, as though he rarely ventured outside into the sun. She was *reminded* of the white underside of a lizard. The man was in a short-sleeved plaid shirt and jeans. He held a notebook and pen in his hands.

"Ah might have known y'all'd be hangin' 'round here," Governor Roy said in a weary tone.

The man just smiled.

"This, Miz Dwah'yer, is Terrance Sylvestor, of the *Courier*."

"A journalist, then." She paused, then said, "I'm Kate Dwyer."

"How charmed I am," the man said. "Are you here because of the governor's bid for reelection?"

"No," the woman replied truthfully.

28

"You're part of the campaign then." He looked her up and down, noting her well-developed breasts, the curve of her hips in her jeans, the tucked-in waist. "A helper," he said snidely.

"What, then, is your capacity?"

She ignored the sexual innuendo and looked him straight in the eye, blue eyes meeting brown ones. "Actually, Mr. Sylvestor, that's none of your business. Now, if you'll excuse us." Distasteful as it was, she took the governor's arm and walked away.

As they approached the governor's office, the burly man shook his head. "That reporter sure is my nexus."

Nemesis, thought Kate, but didn't say a word. How could she correct a man who thought "symphony" and "sympathy" were interchangeable?

Once they were back in his office, Kate said, "All right, you want me to leave as soon as possible. How about tomorrow?"

He nodded. "That would be fine, Miz Dwah'yer. Guess y'all'd better watch that news hound out there. If he sniffs a story of some kahnd, he'll run it to the ground as quick as a coyote after a lamb." He moved some papers on his desk, then looked up at the young woman again. "Ah have some more reports."

She waited.

"Diner down by White Sands was destroyed last night. The sheriff's office down there reports it was horrible. Apparently happened durin' the wind last night. No one knows what caused it, but all the people in the diner are dead, some of 'em half-eaten."

"My God," she whispered.

"'Course," he went on, oblivious to her expression, "it could be the desert scavengers. Then Ah have this other report." He nodded with his chin. "From a ranch wife down there whose husband called her. She heard this loud hissin', like air escapin' a tire, and then the line went dead. She hasn't seen him since. That was early this mornin'."

"Do you think they're connected, these incidents?"

"Dr. Dwah'yer, at this point Ah cain't believe they're not. And ah got some more reports of cattle mutilations."

"I thought those were mainly in the northern part of the state," Kate said.

"Most of them earlier reports have been," the governor said, scowling. "But the ones from the south are a bit different. These cattle are killed outright and partially eaten. Lot of 'em are disappearin'. 'Course we suspect rustlers, as well. But them cows that have been found was flattened, jes' like a steamroller went over 'em." He studied the woman. "For Gawd's sake, Miz Dwah'yer, y'all gotta find out what's goin' on down there."

Chapter 6

The train's whistle pierced the stillness of the desert night. Its single light, cutting through the blackness, swept in front of the train speeding along the rails.

Hal Mondragon, Governor Roy's political manager, opened his leather briefcase and fished around in the contents for a sheaf of papers held together by a jumbo paper clip. He pushed aside pens and pencils, campaign buttons, and rolled-up papers and charts, and at last found what he was looking for.

He carefully pulled off the paper clip, then attached it to his coat pocket so he wouldn't lose it.

Mondragon scanned the pages quickly. More votes than he had thought were promised from Chaves County this year. Of course, the big cut in the federal aid bill had helped. Last campaign the governor had had trouble with the people there. Some journalist had got hold of a damaging story, something about vetoing a flood-relief bill to the county.

Damned hicks, Mondragon thought irritably. A man bred in the city, he despised those who lived in the country, yet recognized the crucial part they played in New Mexico politics, the state being for the most part a rural one. Still, even if he had to recognize the ranchers' and farmers' usefulness at the polls, that didn't mean he had to personally like them.

And after being with them, in the heart of their land, for two weeks, he was more than ready to get back to civilization.

Roy had selected Mondragon, a graduate of the University of New Mexico Law School, for a number of reasons. Hal Mondragon was a good-looking Chicano, a man whose appearance was faintly reminiscent of the Spanish conquistadors. He had been at the top of his class for three years, on the Dean's List, had practiced law in an old established Albuquerque firm, and, after five years, had grown restless for a challenge. He'd hung out his own shingle and had made more than a comfortable living. He was a go-getter, of that there could be no doubt, but he wasn't an ambulance chaser.

He'd gone to the governor, when the man had still been a state senator and was first beginning to make political noises, and Hal had offered his services, in whatever way possible. For the first two campaigns Mondragon had worked in a legal capacity, and then after Roy's political campaign manager quit last fall to work for the other party, Roy had tapped Mondragon for the job.

He was good, efficient, and dirty—exactly the qualities necessary for the state's politics.

Hal closed his eyes as the printed pages swam in front of him, and leaned back against the seat in the train. He'd been up since four that morning and had already made ten stops through the southern part of the state. All the little whistle-stops and milk runs and there were a lot of them. Tonight he was heading north, and tomorrow they would stop at the towns between Alamogordo and Albuquerque. The following day they would reach Albuquerque, and then it was on to Santa Fe. And home. And his wife. A very lovely, very Anglo woman, from a very wealthy family. He smiled.

He preferred to take the train, for though it wasn't as fast as a plane, he found he could do more work on it and could have time to rest as well.

And there wouldn't be much rest for him or for anyone else involved in Bubba Roy's reelection campaign during the seven weeks remaining until the election.

Seven weeks, and there was still so much to do. Too much. Where would he find the time? He yawned, knuckling his eyes. Now there seemed to be some problems in the southern part of the state. Just what Bubba did not need right now.

Hal stared out at the moonlit landscape. Along the track, beyond the line of telephone poles, he saw a flickering of yellow light.

He watched as it faded into the distance, small and dim and remote. He shrugged. Hoboes and their camp fires, Mondragon decided.

He thought he'd turn out the overhead light and get some shut-eye. After all, it was going to be a long day tomorrow. And the day after … and the day after *that*, and …

Hal Mondragon closed his eyes again and was asleep.

Juan Hipólito Diego leaned back and scratched his paunch. He belched, then took another swig of beer from the can he held in his hand. Absently he tied the white laces of his worn brown-leather shoes.

His companion, Melvin Jones, rummaged through the old canvas pack on the ground between the two men. "Wha'd you bring?" he asked.

"*Frijoles*," Diego said, belching again.

"Hey, excuse you, you *pendejo*," Jones said indignantly.

"'Scuse me," said Diego as he wiped his mouth on his dirty sleeve. He scratched his knee where the material was torn. He got up, stretched, then reached down and hitched up his pants, three sizes too large for him, which were supported by a cord of wrapping string.

"Beans again?" Jones asked. "When you gonna get somethin' different?"

Diego shrugged. "It's all I could find, man. I got it from a trailer. What you got?"

Jones pulled out a packet of slightly crumpled aluminum foil. He carefully unfolded the foil to reveal four wrinkled hot dogs. He held them to his nose one by one. Slightly old, but still good.

He handed two of the wieners to Diego, who put them on a long stick. Both hoboes set the sticks over the open campfire. Jones opened the can of beans, then placed it in the warm coals. They watched as the wieners turned brown, and the flames leaped up as the meat juices dripped into the fire.

The light of their fire reflected off the cement of the culvert in which they had camped. Above them, on the level ground, the wind whistled, bringing with it the moist scent of distant rain. But down in the culvert the two hoboes were protected from the elements.

The beans were soon warmed up, and the two men began eating the stolen food. Jones got out a wine bottle, uncorked it, and passed it to Diego after he'd had a swig. They ate in companionable silence.

Jones burped, then stretched out flat on his back so that he could stare at the stars overhead.

This was certainly the life, he told himself. Sure beat working in the city for some hard-ass boss who was going to underpay a guy, no matter how much work he did. He yawned. It'd been so simple to leave, too, that old life. Just got up one morning, packed his lunch, went to the factory and looked at his boss, some transplanted Texan with boots that cost more than he got paid in a week, told him to shove it, and left.

He hadn't been back since then, and that had been how long? Six, seven years ago?

For a fleeting moment Jones thought of his young wife and the daughter he'd left behind in Portales.

Then the memory, the ache was gone. That had been too long ago. She'd be remarried, no doubt; the kid would have another father, would have long since forgotten him. It didn't matter anymore. He was free.

"Hey, man, I gotta go piss," Diego said. He stumbled to his feet and held his crotch. He made his way along the culvert until he came to a worn place where he found purchase and scrambled up the side. He looked around for a likely bush.

In the culvert below, Melvin Jones continued to lie with his hands behind his head. The sand was soft beneath him, softer than any mattress had ever been. He listened to the howl of the wind, moaning through the sand beyond the culvert.

He puckered his lips and whistled an old tune, one that he and the kid used to sing together. He brushed back a strand of dirty hair and stretched with his arms far over his head.

It felt good, real good.

Minutes passed, and he waited for Diego to return. He dozed, and when he awoke a little later with a start, he realized the other man still hadn't returned. Then over the shriek of the desert wind, Jones heard a scream, faint, as if blown away by the wind.

Jones sat up and looked around, blinking. "Hey, Juan?" he called. "Juan!"

There was no answer except the moaning of the wind. And then:

Hiss. Hiss.

The hissing filled his head, growing even louder than the wind, and he put his hands over his ears to keep the sound out of his brain. Panicked, wondering what it could be, wondering what could have happened to Diego, Jones looked up at the edge of the cement culvert.

Jones screamed, backing away in the sand, not even bothering, not remembering, to get to his feet.

For above him were two legs, the feet shod with brown-leather shoes with white laces, and the legs protruded from the mouth of a

35

giant lizard. Yellow eyes, hateful, baleful, glared down at him, and the creature slowly moved toward the edge of the culvert. Toward Jones.

He screamed again and again.

Chapter 7

The Golden Palomino Motel in Torres, Otero County, wasn't the finest in hotel accommodations, Kate decided, but by the look of the rest of the small town it was certainly the best available.

She'd flown in that afternoon, after making arrangements for two other instructors to take over her three classes while she was in the southern part of the state. She'd consulted the AAA for recommendations on a motel, but either Torres was too small to warrant the rating of any hotel facilities, or it was that bad.

She preferred to think it was the former.

The Golden Palomino was a cluster of rambling stucco buildings spray-painted a garish pink. It was supposed to look like authentic adobe; it failed. Wooden shutters, painted an off-shade green, framed the windows, and outside each bungalow, which was protected from insect life by a bulged-out screen door, was a small patch of long grass in which sat a white-and-green metal lawn chair.

She walked to the office with her small overnight case and set about getting a room. Behind the desk, the manager—large, florid, with bad teeth, stained and rather long and yellow like a horse's— smiled ingratiatingly at her. Kate ignored him, signed the register, and left the bill open, not knowing how long she would be there.

Once in her bungalow, she set her case down and looked around. A double bed squatted in the center of one wall, sagging alarmingly in the middle. It was covered with a red chenille bedspread, and it appeared that former occupants of the room had had plenty of time on their hands. The spread was bald in places, the tufts having been plucked out.

A wooden chair with a leather cushion stood next to the bed, as did a scarred nightstand. Opposite the bed was a long lightwood dresser with a mirror that had dimmed with age. A small lamp, its parchment shade decorated with scenes of the Wild West, was next to the bed. An accordion door hid a closet large enough for four hangers.

The bathroom was even worse. Reflexively Kate curled her toes in her shoes as she stared at the stained tile floor and thought about crossing it in her bare feet. The tub and basin were white and cracked and bore yellowish stains. A half-opened window was propped up with a piece of wood, and dirt was caked along the sill.

She washed her face and neck to remove some of the sweat from traveling, then changed clothing. She put on comfortable jeans, sturdy shoes, and a lightweight sweater. She wanted to get to the sheriff's office and go out to the scene of the bus wreck as soon as possible.

As she walked along the main street of Torres, heading toward the sheriff's office, she saw a group of young men lounging alongside a building, just inside a line of shade. They stared unabashed at her and a couple of them whistled.

Knowing what was coming, Kate averted her head and stared across the narrow street.

"*Hey, señorita,*" one called.

"You got somethin' to show me, baby?"

"*Chica, chica!*"

"Pussycat!"

"Hey, c'mon over here, honey, *I* got somethin' to show to *you!*"

"Whyn't you come right over here, little one, I show you—"

"Hey, shake 'em, baby, you won't break 'em!"

The catcalls in English and Spanish, the whistles continued as she approached the men. Her Spanish was good enough to understand what they were saying, and a dull flush rose from her neck, spreading over her face.

Damned men, she thought bitterly. Why a woman couldn't walk down a street without being subjected to vocal harassment she didn't know. Here she was, a well-known herpetologist, a professor at the largest university in the state, and she was being persecuted by these small-town creeps, a bunch of hoods.

Kate, get a hold of yourself, she said silently, and drew her lips together in a thin line.

The rude calls continued as she walked past the men; she kept her pace steady, resolving that she would not allow them the satisfaction of seeing her run away.

One of the men broke away from the group, and she could sense him following at a distance.

"Hey," he called.

Kate ignored him. God alone knew what he would try to say to her if she stopped!

"Hey, Doctor," he called.

The woman frowned at that, but turned a deaf ear to him. She wouldn't stop.

"Hey," he shouted a third time, and Kate could hear him running toward her.

Finally she could take it no longer. The woman whirled, her hands on her hips, a frown on her face.

"Now, look, buddy—" she began furiously, then stopped as she stared at the man's dark face. "Chato Del-Klinne," she said, disbelief on her face.

The full-blooded Chiricahua Apache grinned at her and gave her a mock bow. "None other."

"What the hell are you doing here?" she demanded. "And," with sudden suspicion, "were you making rude comments along with those other guys back there?"

A sheepish look passed over the man's bronze face, tinging his high cheekbones. "Shake 'em, baby, you won't break 'em,'" he repeated ruefully, trying hard not to grin.

"I ought to break you," she cried, but her blue eyes were laughing.

"Hey, lady," he said, affecting a heavy accent, "I show you a good time."

As she looked at her former colleague, Kate thought that he probably could. He was of medium height, but lean and hard-muscled, and his hands looked as though they had seen a lot of outdoor work. They weren't the soft white hands of an office man, the sort of hands she disliked. His long black hair was neatly gathered at the nape of his neck with a tan cloth, and his sparkling black eyes were smiling at her. He wore clean blue jeans, boots, and a rust-colored Navajo velvet shirt. In fact, she thought, he looked damned good.

"You haven't finished answering me," Kate said.

"Where the hell have you been these past three years?"

"Oh, yeah"—he shrugged—"well, after I quit my job at the university, I bummed around for a while—"

"Discovering your heritage?" she asked wryly.

"Yeah. Then I hired out as a cowhand."

"A what?"

"You heard me, Kate. A cowhand."

"You worked steers, and roped, and that whole thing?" she asked with rising disbelief in her voice.

"It's a living, and an honest one, too," he said without any rancor. "But right now I'm between jobs—unless you got some cows you want me to wrestle to the ground."

"No, thanks!"

"Hey," Chato said suddenly, "you want to go to dinner with me, Kate?"

"I can't today," Kate said, feeling genuine disappointment. "I have to go to the sheriff's office and I don't know how long I'll be there. But what about rain-checking it until tomorrow?"

"Okay. I know where you live, lady, so don't worry." He grinned at her again, and she found herself responding.

"Good seeing you again, Chato."

"Yeah, same for me, Kate."

She waved to him and continued on her way down the street.

Sheriff MacIntyre was a burly man, much like the governor, but friendly, and once she explained that Bubba Roy had sent her to investigate, he offered right away to drive her out to the wreck.

The site was about ten miles beyond the town, on a barely paved road. On the way there the sheriff filled Kate in on the wreck. Once there, Kate clambered down the side of the arroyo and gazed at the fine sand on the bottom. New sediment lay over older sand, and she could see that just recently the arroyo had been a torrent.

Chato would have been at home, she thought wryly. He could have looked at all the rocks and strata to his heart's content.

The wreckage had been removed already, but here and there Kate found bits of twisted metal. She walked along the bottom of the arroyo and scuffed the sand with her foot. Something glittered in the sand, and she stooped to pick it up.

It was a small medal on a chain. The Virgin Mary. She thought of the high school kids who had been killed in the wreck. Except for two of them. Both were still in the hospital, but things didn't look too good for either one. MacIntyre had told her that the boy, the school's punter, stood to lose both legs, while the head cheerleader's caved-in rib cage had punctured one lung and the doctors were battling to save her life. Both had been flown to Albuquerque for the medical facilities there.

She walked farther along the arroyo, staring at the ground. She had no reason to believe she would find anything that would give her a clue to the reptile that had fallen with the bus, but there might be something.

She turned back briefly to look at the sheriff some distance away. He probably thought she was crazy—just walking up and down the arroyo. "City folk," she could hear him say, shaking his head.

She smiled and continued to search.

Without warning, she fell to her knees and dug in the sand, the dirt flying all over her. Then she brushed away the grains.

"What'd you find?" the sheriff called, hurrying toward the scientist. He stopped on the eroded lip of the Arroyo Peligroso and stared.

"This," she said, and held up a six-inch-long tooth.

There was a brisk knock at the door of her bungalow. She opened the door and found Chato leaning there.

"Hi," he said. "Brought you a six-pack."

The Indian pushed past her and set the carton on the scarred surface of the dresser.

She whirled to face him. "Chato! You know I don't drink beer."

"So who said anything about beer?" he responded.

She looked at the six-pack. "Sprite?"

"Sure. I thought we'd have a little drink, celebrate our meeting up again, remember old times."

Kate laughed. "You crazy Apache," she said affectionately.

He stepped across to her, sliding his arms around her. Briefly he nuzzled her red hair.

"I liked old times," Chato murmured.

Her pulse quickening, Kate moved closer to him, so close that she felt the turquoise buckle on his belt press into her flat abdomen. She felt the hardness in his crotch, too. When they had worked at the university, meeting over the copier shared by the biology and geology departments, she had been attracted to the good-looking man with the wry sense of humor. She had wondered at the time whether she'd like him more because he was Chato or because he was the first Indian she'd ever known personally.

She guessed she was about to find out.

They fell onto the bed and quickly pulled off their clothing. Nude, he was as lean and firm as she had imagined. Chato cradled her breasts in his hands and smiled at her.

"They're not … inconsequential. I like that." For emphasis he squeezed them.

"What man doesn't?" She smiled up at him.

"I guess we could talk," Chato said suddenly.

"Talk?" Her reply was startled.

"Yeah. It's been a long time since we've seen each other. We've seen more of the world, had a few more knocks, had a few more—"

"Fucks?" she asked sweetly.

His shocked look was mocking. "My dear lady, that is definitely unladylike language!"

She let her long dark lashes fall over her blue eyes, and she could hear him gasp.

"To hell with drawing-room manners," he growled, and pressed his mouth down on hers. Then his hands were moving all over her soft body, fanning fires like those across a prairie. His hands were skilled, exacting, and made her feel so good. She cried out, demanding that he come into her, and with one fluid motion he entered her and thrust deep. She wiggled under him and laughed as the delicious feelings rolled over her. Over and over she was lifted high on this wave of sensation, until at last, with a muted cry, he came in her.

They lay still for a long time, locked in each other's arms, and then Kate stirred.

"I think I'd like one of those Sprites now, please."

Chato got up and brought back a can, opened it, and handed it to her after taking a swallow. Then he went back to the dresser and stared down at an object lying there.

Returning, he threw himself down with an alarming squeak of the bed's springs.

"I'm surprised we didn't break it," he grunted.

She leaned over and kissed him on the lips. She ran her fingers lightly across his high cheekbones. "We'll have more opportunity later."

He grinned and locked his fingers behind his head. She stroked a strand of black hair off his forehead. Alternately she sipped at the Sprite and held it to his lips.

"Why does that thing on the dresser look like a tooth?" he asked at length, staring up into her blue eyes.

"Because it is," the woman replied.

"You've become a dentist?"

"Hardly." Kate laughed. She yawned, then ran a hand down his side, feeling his ribs. She felt the smoothness of his belly, then her hand trailed downward.

"By the way—um, good—just what the hell are *you* doing here?" Chato demanded. "You were running off to the sheriff's office this afternoon and didn't get back till late this evening."

She stretched and he slipped an arm around her. "You remember that bus that was wrecked a few nights ago?" Chato nodded. "The governor called me the following morning and asked me to come to Santa Fe. Which I did. He had there an object found at the sight of the crash—a tail."

"A tail, huh? I know where to find a tail," he said.

"Don't you dare pinch me," she warned. They both laughed, and he kissed her. "I came down here at his insistence, went to the site, and found the tooth."

"That's one damn big tooth. What of?"

44

"I can't be sure until I return to the university, but I have studied it a little and it appears to be one from a Gila monster. It has the groove for the poison," she explained.

Chato sat up and looked at Kate, astonished. "But Gilas are generally no longer than two to three feet. This tooth is over half a foot long. Why"—he made quick mental estimates—"that means the beast would be at least fifteen feet long!"

Kate took a long swallow of the Sprite, then looked directly in the man's black eyes. "That's right, Chato. And not an inch less. And maybe even longer. I just don't know."

The Indian whistled soundlessly.

"*Brujos*," whispered Eddie Chavez, crossing himself quickly and downing a glass of tequila. "It's the work *of a brujo*."

Jimmy Cannon, leaning against the dark wooden bar alongside Eddie, laughed deeply and clapped the Chicano farmer on the shoulder.

"Obviously, son, you've been drinkin', but just not the right sort of stuff. Barkeep, get this boy some decent likker."

The bartender poured a glass of Scotch and handed it to Chavez, who sipped it and shuddered.

"It's true, Señor Cannon," the young farmer said. "What else could be killing off our cattle?"

"Martians," said a man, coming up to the bar.

"What?" asked a scowling Cannon.

"It's them Martians that've been landin'," the man drawled. He sipped at his glass and sloshed the liquid around as he stared at it. "What else could explain them mutilations? Nothing but Martians, I tell you. Got them big spaceships circlin' the earth. Motherships. Just ready and a-waitin' to come kill us next." He nodded knowledgably at Cannon and Chavez.

"*Brujos*," Chavez repeated, fingering a gold crucifix. His lips moved in a silent entreaty to the Virgin.

"It's not no *brujos* or Martians," Cannon said. "It's just some stray animal that's been goin' after our cattle and killin' 'em."

"You ever see any animal that could rip through a cow that way, the way that the Ortegas' herd was destroyed?" the man asked.

Remembering the corpses as they lay on the ground, half-eaten, their legs smashed beneath them as if something huge had trod on them afterward, Cannon admitted to himself, that he hadn't. Not on this earth, anyway. But it certainly wasn't any Martian monster.

"Nah," he replied casually. "But that don't mean it ain't some critter we don't know nothin' about."

"Like what?" the third man, who introduced himself as Bill Hardy, asked.

"Dunno," Cannon said, waving to the bartender for another fill-up. "But I'll prove it to you."

"How?" Hardy demanded.

"I'll go out there with my shotgun tonight, wait for that critter to show, and then shoot it and bring it back here," Cannon said matter-of-factly.

"Madre de Dios," Chavez said in a low tone. "Don't go, Señor Cannon. Do not be *loco*. Please—I beg you."

"Mebbe I am, mebbe I'm not," the old rancher said. "It a deal?" he asked Hardy.

"You're willing to lay a bet on this?" Hardy asked.

"That's right," Cannon said.

"You *are* crazy!" the other Anglo exclaimed.

"No, just bullheaded, and determined to show the rest of you lily-fisted types that there ain't nothin' to be afraid of. Why," the old man said, patting the shotgun that rested against the barstool to his left, "there ain't nothin' I couldn't bring to its knees with this. Except an elephant, mebbe. Mebbe."

"Twenty-five bucks?" asked Hardy, bringing out a roll and peeling off two tens and a five.

"Yep." Cannon reached in and brought out a twenty and five ones. He laid them on the countertop alongside his drink. "Here, Pancho," he said to the bartender, "you watch after this money."

The man nodded. "*Si, señor.*" He gathered the fifty dollars and placed them in a beer mug behind the counter.

"When will you do it, Señor Cannon?" Eddie Chavez wanted to know.

"Tonight," Cannon replied, downing another drink.

"How'll we know you'll go out there?" Hardy asked.

Cannon looked at him, his white eyebrows drawn together. "Brother, you ain't lived long, 'cause when a Cannon gives his word, he goes by it."

"Okay, okay, no need to get hostile. I just wondered."

"I'll be goin' out tonight." He got up stiffly from the barstool and tossed a few crumpled bills onto the countertop. "That oughta cover my drinks, as well as my friends'."

"*Gracias, señor,*" Chavez said, while Hardy nodded his head toward the white-haired rancher.

Cannon carefully picked up his shotgun and weaved across the tile floor and out the door of the bar.

Chapter 8

As far as he knew that mauraudin' critter made its appearance at night, and by God, he, Jimmy Belirose Cannon, would be there waiting.

Pausing, he checked the gasoline level on his Land Rover. It was over three-quarters full. He'd have to watch out for the battery, though, as it had been giving him some trouble recently. Meant to take it in, of course, but never got around to it. Cannon packed a thermos of coffee, a sack of roast beef sandwiches, a sturdy flashlight, and of course, his shotgun.

After the long ride under the starry night sky, Cannon found a spot to stop his vehicle. He was in the middle of the desert, well off any heavily traveled roads and far from any town. There were no houses nearby, and it was just Jimmy Cannon and the cattle out there in the quiet night.

He poured a cup of coffee and looked around at the moonlit landscape.

The shadows gave the common objects—the rocks, the mesquite, the cacti—weird shapes, and some seemed poised to leap on the unwary. A low wind moaned across the desert floor, and the herd of cattle before him moved, stamping their feet, lowing, making all the sounds the stupid beasts usually made.

It hadn't been hard to find a spot to park. After all, he'd simply taken a look at a map and seen where the five attacks on the cattle had been. The first had been in the southern part of the county, and the most recent had been about ten miles southeast of his present location. Anyone with an eye and a brain in his head could tell that creature was moving northward.

He shifted in the Land Rover's seat, stretching out his long legs so that they wouldn't cramp. It might be a long wait. That critter might not show up tonight. Didn't have to. In fact, he couldn't see that it had made a regular appearance. It was just … well, tonight he had a feeling.

Cannon glanced up at the moon, a pale yellow, and it seemed to grin down at him. Nights like this, the *nativos* here said, strange things happened. *Brujos*, they would say.

He shook his head. He was listening to them damned Mexicans too much, getting his head filled with their superstitious nonsense about witches and the like. Then there was that Hardy fellow with his idiotic notion about motherships and bug-eyed Martians.

Bunch of bullshit, all of it, Cannon grumbled to himself.

Standing up in the Rover, Cannon picked up his binoculars and made a sweep of the landscape. Nothing but sand and mesquite and tumbleweeds.

He pulled out a sandwich and began eating it. As his teeth ripped at the meat, he thought of how the area had changed since he and Emma had first come here.

Must have been … he paused in his chewing to calculate. He was seventy-two, and he'd been twenty-six then. Why, it'd been forty-six years since they'd come to Otero County. Hadn't been a thing here then. Just some ol' tumbleweeds and cacti, and a building or two. Otero had a few more people now, but it really hadn't changed that much. Except the desert wasn't as quiet as it'd been in those days. It was those teenagers driving every which way on the desert; didn't care what they ran over, or what happened.

Pouring himself another cup of coffee, he yawned and knuckled his eyes. He stretched again, hearing vertebrae snap back into place.

The cows jostled around the Rover in pairs, and stared in at the human. They continued their aimless wandering.

He was feeling mighty tired. He thought he'd just tip his hat back and lean his head on the seat for a minute, just rest a few seconds or so, and then ...

When he woke, he was cold and stiff. He moved with difficulty, uncapping the Thermos for another cup of coffee. It wasn't as warm as it'd been earlier, and he wondered what time it was. He glanced at his wristwatch. The luminous numerals read 12:04. He yawned. He must have been asleep for about two hours.

Cannon stepped out of the Rover to relieve himself, and when he returned, he paused before climbing in again.

What was that sound?

He cocked his head, trying to hear the noise over the wind, trying to identify it. Sounded like ... like ... He shook his head. He must be hearing things. Hissing for God's sake?

Cannon glanced around and the cattle were milling nervously.

Hiss. Hiss.

Something black blotted out the light to the south and he stared.

It was coming his way.

The cattle started to move away.

Not knowing what propelled him, Cannon got into the Rover. Suddenly it was surrounded by panic-stricken cattle. They pressed around the vehicle, and it rocked with the force. Suddenly the unidentifiable sound became identifiable.

It *was* hissing.

Cannon turned his head to look back over his shoulder, and his mouth flew open at what he saw.

The cattle were now stampeding, buffeting the Land Rover, and the night air was filled with the sounds of terrified cattle and that awful sound, that *hissing*.

Cannon turned the key in the ignition, and the engine missed. Damned thing. He tried again, and it failed. He floorboarded the Land Rover, and he realized he'd just flooded the engine.

Damn! Helpless, he struck the steering wheel with a fist, and listened, his heart pounding, as the sound came closer and closer. The cattle were running down the desert floor, away from the creature—creatures that crawled toward them ... toward him.

He waited for what seemed an eternity and then tried the engine again. With a rusty growl it sprang into life. His heart still pounding, the old rancher released the hand brake and accelerated the Land Rover. It leaped from where it had sat for hours.

Behind him came the hissing, louder and louder and louder.

He pushed the accelerator down and left the nightmares behind.

He drove wildly, the pounding in his chest coming into his ears now, and he barely missed going off the road several times. Shooting pains, tingling like pinpricks, radiated through his chest and his left arm, and he had to blink rapidly to see.

He had to get away, had to tell the others in town what he had seen, what was killing their cattle.

It was far worse than they'd imagined.

The phone was ringing, and Kate rolled over, pretending it was just a very loud and persistent cricket. But the noise would not go away. She started to put her head under the pillow to keep the sound out.

"Phone," mumbled Chato by her side.

"You get it."

"No, you get it. It's by you."

Slowly, without opening her eyes, she reached across to the nightstand. She wondered what time it was. "Hello?"

"Dr. Dwyer?"

"Yes." Kate swallowed so she could speak better.

"This is Dr. Martinez at the Otero County Health Clinic. We have a patient here we think you ought to see."

She sat up, the sheet sliding to her hips. "A patient I ought to see?' she repeated. She looked over at Chato in the moonlight. He was wide awake with a questioning look on his dark face.

"Sheriff's office told us to get in touch with you," the doctor said. "It's an emergency, ma'am."

"Very well, I'll be there as soon as I can get dressed."

She put the phone down on its cradle and looked at the Apache. "Well, don't be lazy. Get up and get dressed. I'm not the only one who's going to suffer from lack of sleep."

Chato grinned in response.

Within twenty minutes they had dressed and gone to the small two-doctor clinic on the east side of town.

Dr. Alan Martinez was tall, with tapering surgeon's fingers. Kate thought he looked like one of the figure out of an El Greco painting. Very lean, pale, ascetic. There was something almost holy about his appearance.

"This way, please," the doctor said after they had introduced themselves. His eyes had flicked briefly the first time Chato had spoken, and Kate wondered at the reaction. Was it because Chato was Apache? Surely the doctor had treated Indians before. But, she thought, restraining a yawn, that didn't mean he liked them. Suddenly the doctor looked a whole lot less holy.

They passed through the emergency room and went into one of the cubicles. On one side was a cloth screen that reached no higher than five feet. Sheriff MacIntyre stood by the bed in which an old Anglo man lay. Kate moved forward when the sheriff beckoned to her.

"This here is Jimmy Cannon. Rancher here," the sheriff said. "He was out lookin' for that creature that'd been destroyin' the cattle herds in these parts. He came weavin' into town about an hour ago, smashed his Rover into the window of Pancho's bar-and-grill. He's been babblin' ever since about what he saw out there."

"Eyes … eyes … big and yellow," the old man whispered, then grimaced as a barb of pain shot through him.

"Mr. Cannon, my name is Kate Dwyer. I'm from the university in Albuquerque. Please, sir, could you tell what you saw this evening?"

His eyes focused for a moment, her words apparently reaching him through the pain, and he moved his hand. She took the gnarled hand in hers, and felt the viselike grip. He was sick, perhaps even dying, but he was still a strong man.

"Emma," he said. "Emma."

The woman glanced across at the sheriff. "Emma was his wife," MacIntyre explained. "She died last year, after a series of strokes."

Kate nodded, then turned her attention back to the old rancher.

"Yellow eyes." He sobbed, his own closed tightly. Tears squeezed out of them and ran down the crevices of his sun-wrinkled skin.

"Mr. Cannon, what did you see tonight?"

He moved his lips, but she couldn't hear a word. She was aware that the other men stood watching her. Kate leaned down, placing her ear close to Cannon's lips, and listened. He coughed, and she straightened.

"That's all, please," Dr. Martinez said, coming up to them. "You must go now. My patient needs rest."

"Mr. Cannon," Kate said, her dark eyebrows drawn together, "are you sure that's what you saw?"

"Saw 'em … saw 'em … big as trucks … black and orange … and those eyes!" He cried out, and she jacked away with alarm. "Those eyes," he said over and over.

Hastily she left the cubicle, idly noting that Chato was leaning on the night nurse's desk, chatting with the woman. He saw Kate and straightened, a somewhat sheepish expression on his face.

Kate waited until he came over. "What's wrong?" Chato asked, taking in the look on her face. "What was so important?"

Kate rubbed a hand over her face and sighed. It was so incredible. It couldn't be true ... not really. But the old man said he saw them. Said he saw them, the words echoed in her mind. "That old man saw something tonight in the desert." She paused.

"What?" Chato pressed.

At that moment Dr. Martinez came out of the cubicle and joined the couple. "I'm afraid Mr. Cannon is dead. He lapsed into a coma and just slid away. It was a massive heart attack."

"I hope that I didn't contribute to it," Kate said with concern.

The doctor shook his head. "No, no. He would have died anyway. He had a long history of heart ailments, and tonight, well, tonight was simply too much strain."

Sheriff MacIntyre moved alongside the doctor. "How'm I goin' to label this?" he asked.

"Simply heart attack, I would say," Dr. Martinez replied, and the sheriff nodded.

Chato drew Kate away from the two men and looked closely at her. "What did the old man see?" he demanded, his black eyes bright with curiosity.

Her face, when she lifted it to look at him, was drawn into serious lines.

"He saw"—she paused—"he saw giant Gila monsters."

Chapter 9

On returning to Albuquerque, Kate went directly to her lab at the university. Chato, who had come with her, wandered through the various offices, leafed through numerous magazines, and drank soft drinks while Kate worked.

He glanced at the clock on the wall. Not even noon yet. Kate had wanted to return to the city as soon as possible, so they had packed early that morning and left on a chartered plane. He had gone with her, as he really had no reason to stay down in Torres. He was between jobs anyway.

He had gone next door to the geology department to greet old colleagues. They had all been eager to hear what he had been doing, but once he told them, they had simply stared at him in amazement. Not many Ph.D. geologists dropped everything to become cowboys. He could well imagine that thought turning over and over in their minds. As he walked through the old familiar hallways, saw the same people, the same things, he thought of the classes he had taught, the students, and didn't regret leaving the university. He had enjoyed them, but it had been a trap, an office job, and he much preferred what he was doing now. He wasn't making spectacular money as a cowhand, but he got to be outside in the sun and the fresh air. And the rain and snow and wind and dust, he thought wryly.

He walked outside the biology department, where he'd been waiting for Kate the last two hours, put two quarters in the soft-drink machine, and pushed a button. The can rolled down; he opened it and took a long drink, drifting back toward Kate's office.

He had always marveled at how someone so neat in her personal appearance could maintain so messy an office. Stacks of paper were on her desk, beside it, in front of it. They covered the bookcases and the metal file cabinets, and everywhere he looked he saw more paper.

Books were stacked on their sides, crossways in the bookcases, on a table, even on her chair. He smiled as he lifted the stacks of books there, sat, and leaned back, resting his feet on the desktop. He continued sipping the soft drink and stared across at her large Sierra Club calendar. On a shelf to his left a small gecko lizard rustled in its cage.

The door of the lab flew open and Kate, a white coat over her street clothes, emerged with a sheaf of notes in one hand. She looked slightly harried ... and decidedly beautiful and desirable, Chato thought.

"Hi," she said absently. "Thought I'd find you here."

"You did," Chato said. "Want a sip?"

"What?" She looked up from her notes. "No, thanks."

"What's up? Did you find out what that tooth belonged to?"

She nodded as she perched on the edge of the desk. Her feet swung clear of the floor, and he gazed at her ankles. Nice and neat and trim. He felt a stirring inside him. God, he must be horny if he was getting turned on by the sight of a woman's ankles!

"You're not going to believe this."

"I don't know about that," Chato said, forcing his eyes to her face.

"I was correct, down in Torres," the woman said. "It *is* a tooth from a Gila monster."

He whistled soundlessly. "They just don't grow that large, Kate. Could this be some sort of hoax? Maybe some college kids planted the tooth after the cattle mutilations down there. That sort of thing has happened before." His black eyes gazed at her speculatively as he swallowed some more soft drink.

"I've considered that. But, no, it's real enough. I checked right away, and it's all too authentic. And it just confirms what poor old Mr. Cannon said. Giant Gila monsters."

"Yeah, but how?" Chato asked. "I mean, this old guy says he saw these creatures, and you find this tooth—"

"And don't forget there was that chunk of charred tail. I matched tissues from that with those of the Gila," Kate said.

"Okay, then, but I still want to know how? How did these buggers grow to this size? And isn't there some law or something of physics that says you can't grow things too big. I can't remember precisely what it *does* say."

"Well, size doesn't affect a Komodo dragon, or an elephant, and the dinosaurs did all right … for a while." Kate smiled.

"But—"

"I know," she said slowly. Picking up a pencil, she thoughtfully tapped it against the shade of the gooseneck lamp on her desk. Chato leaned over, took the pencil from her and placed it in a drawer.

"The tissues match," she went on, "but the hide outside is different."

"How different?" he asked.

"It's harder. More like scaly armor." She ran a hand through her hair. "It has to be a mutation. And it must be a result of the nuclear radiation from the Trinity Site. There can't be any other explanation."

"Trinity," he said slowly, and remembered what he had heard, what he had read. In 1945 the first atomic device had been exploded near White Sands at the Trinity Site. It had seemed, at that time, in the midst of the desert, nothing more than a large and powerful bomb. It had been only much later, too late for Hiroshima and Nagasaki, that the atomic bomb had been found to be more than "just" a bomb.

"That was over thirty-five years ago," the herpetologist mused aloud. "Think of the countless generations of lizards as they grew larger and larger, the smaller ones down there dying off or being eaten by the others."

"How did they survive undetected all these years?" Chato asked.

The woman shrugged. "Who knows? Except that it's still not very populous there. Lots of desert and sand, and they could miss being noticed."

"And maybe," Chato said, "they just recently reached a size where they might be noticed."

"That could well be." She leaned over to take a sip from his drink. Her lab coat fell open and he could see the swell of her breasts under her beige blouse. *Nice firm breasts, too,* he thought, and remembered the night before in the motel.

As if sensing what he was thinking, she blushed slightly.

"What next?" he asked.

"I want to get these notes tied, correlate them, and then do some more thinking."

"Lunch?"

"Of course, and then later we'll go to dinner, and sometime in there I'll call the governor and let him know what I've found."

"Dinner, eh?"

"My treat," Kate said smiling, "at my place."

He grinned. "I won't refuse."

"I never saw your apartment before," Chato said as he lay on his back and stared up at the oyster-white ceiling, then glanced around Kate's bedroom. Decorated in subtle earth tones, the roof reflected the Southwest culture. Her entire apartment was designed to blend Indian and Spanish motifs. How different it was from his own home down south. He and his parents and brother had lived in a one-bedroom wood house, and the bathroom had been out in the back. Later, when he was a teenager, they had gotten running water. Funny, when he'd lived there, he'd never thought of himself as being particularly deprived.

"Beats living in a tepee," she replied casually.

"Wickiup," he corrected automatically. "Apaches traditionally live in wickiups." He continued, "I never lived—" Glancing over at her, he saw the laughter in her blue eyes. "Why, you little fiend!" Rolling over onto her, he kissed her.

She trailed a hand down his spine and caressed his buttocks.

Chato kissed her cheek; his mouth slid to her neck, down to her breasts, down to her waist.

She rolled over on top of him, straddling him, and laughed. "Now, I've got you," she said triumphantly, stroking his chest with her long fingers.

"Yeah, but in a minute, I'm going to have you." And he gave a powerful thrust.

Kate moaned, twisting her hips, grinding them down on him. He arched his back, their flesh became one, and he could feel her warmth, spreading out over him, enveloping him. Suddenly he was on top again, and he covered her face and neck with kisses.

She ran her hands through his hair, gripped his back, as he sought to delve deeper. Her legs wound around him, pulling him closer. The fire spread throughout him, and then his release came, and with it his cry of ecstasy.

She smiled into his dark eyes as he stared down at her.

"I never made it with an Indian before."

"I never made it with an Anglo before," he responded.

"Bullshit," she said, smiling at him. "I bet you had them crawling all over you."

"Well," he began, "to be rather modest about it, there were several thousand in college who just threw themselves at me unmercifully."

"Several thousand, huh?"

"That's right. Well, maybe a few hundred—at least a dozen," he said, smiling.

She laughed and hugged him close, and their lips found each other and clung greedily. He could feel the tendrils of lust curling inside him again. Then she pushed him away.

"No, no, not now. Gotta make dinner and call the governor." She rose in one fluid motion from the bed and pulled on a green-and-white-striped caftan.

"I'm gonna loll around for a few minutes longer," he said drowsily, his eyes half-shut. "I never had it so good in my wickiup."

He heard the soft whisper of the bedroom door closing, and then was asleep. When he awoke a little later, he smelled food. His stomach grumbled. He got up, showered, and dressed in his jeans. Pulling his hair back, he secured it, then decided not to pull on his high-topped buckskin moccasins. Too warm, and he liked the feel of her carpet against his toes, anyway.

He walked out of the bedroom and down the hall to the kitchen. It, too, had the Southwestern theme, with a string of red chili peppers by the window and clusters of Indian corn by the door.

Kate was on the phone, the receiver cradled under her chin, and she was standing before the stove, stirring something in a wok. She smiled, winked, and put her hand over the mouthpiece.

"My, we're dressing formally for dinner tonight, I see." She turned back as apparently someone spoke to her over the phone.

He growled and crept up on her, encircling her narrow waist with his hands. They roamed in front and tickled her.

"White woman," he murmured in her ear, and stroked her breasts, which thrust against the material of the caftan.

60

She stifled a giggle from the tickling and motioned him away. Shrugging, Chato looked into the wok, decided he didn't know what it was in it but it certainly looked good, then sat down and began reading the evening paper.

There were several related articles about the cattle mutilations down south. Another one, on the editorial page, asked why a woman professor at the university had gone to see the governor and the following day had been seen in Otero County. Chato wondered if Kate had seen the article yet.

She hung up the phone. "That was the governor's office," she said, dishing out the Chinese vegetables.

"What did our honorable governor have to say for himself?"

"He was interested in what *I* had to say. But I'm not sure that he believes me," Kate said. She stirred her vegetables with a fork.

"Him." His voice was filled with disgust. "He couldn't find his—"

"That's okay," she said. "We both know he's as dumb as a fox." They finished their meal in silence.

Chato got up from the table and went into the bathroom off the hall. As he opened the toilet, he glanced over at the tub, then hastily backed out.

"Kate!" he yelled. "Kate! Come here, quick!"

"What is it?" She came running down the hall.

He nodded toward the bathroom, and she glanced in. Her face relaxed. "Oh. Don't you like chameleons?"

"Not in the bathtub," he said. "And not when I don't know they're there."

She took his hand and led him back in. He watched as the small lizards crawled around in the enamel bathtub and scrabbled at the sides.

"They're too small to climb out yet. And it's easy to keep them in there."

"Wish you'd warned me," he muttered.

61

"I'm glad you're not squeamish," she said, but there was a note of amusement in her voice. "I have to feed my snakes now."

"Snakes?"

"Come with me."

She led him out into the living room, where he sat on the beige-and-sienna couch.

"Snakes. Those cages." She pointed. Under the windowsill was a row of cages that he had somehow overlooked when he'd first come in. He supposed he'd had other things on his mind, and he grinned, remembering.

She went into one room and came out with a shoebox. From inside came the sound of frantic scrambling. Kate knelt, opened the top of the cage, and took off the lid of the shoebox. Out poked a small nose.

"Mice," she said, before Chato could open his mouth.

"I can't watch," he said, and he fell back on the couch, dragging a cream-colored pillow over his face.

At least, he thought, the snakes were quiet about eating those poor mice, and they didn't make horrible munching sounds.

"All finished," she said at last. "I thought Indians liked nature and animals and were attuned to that sort of stuff."

He looked out with a wary eye. "Not this Indian!"

She left the room, washed her hands, and returned. "I've given it a lot of thought," she said, sitting on the couch. She ran her fingers along the smooth skin of his flat belly.

Involuntarily his muscles tightened and he could feel the tingling in his groin. "And?" he prompted.

"I've got to go back to Otero County."

He grabbed her hand and kissed the palm. "Why?"

"I have to see one of those Gilas."

"You're crazy."

"Crazy or not, I'm going."

"Yeah?"

"Yeah."

Chato sighed deeply, pulling her face down to his.

"Well, then count me in, lady. Where you go, I go. Your faithful Indian scout or something like that."

"Good." And she kissed him.

And just maybe, he thought, nothing would happen to them. Maybe. If they were lucky.

Chapter 10

The blackness came again, and he pushed the wheelbarrow around on the gravel, crunching it underneath. He pushed the wheelbarrow and pushed it. Because they had told him. A long time ago.

Around in a circle he went, each foot making a crunching sound as he moved first the left, then the right foot. Then came the wheelbarrow. *Crunch.*

Around and around. Around and around. Around and around. For hours. For days. Weeks. Months.

Around and around.

He had a name. And if he thought hard, he could remember it. He wrinkled his forehead. He smacked his palm against his forehead, just the way he had seen it on the TV. The idiot tube, they called it. Grinning, he drooled.

Around and around.

Oh, *si*, his name. His name. Around and around. *Crunch.* His name. Around and around.

Epi—? What? What? Epi—be couldn't remember. It didn't matter.

Around and around.

Crunch, crunch, crunch.

A new sound was added to the crunching underfoot. *Hiss.*

Crunch, crunch, hiss, crunch.

Crunch, hiss, hiss, crunch, hiss.

Hiss, hiss, crunch, hiss, hiss.

He stopped the wheelbarrow. He looked up and blinked through watery eyes. He rubbed his hand across his nose.

"Kitty, kitty," he called. "Here, kitty, kitty, kitty." He grinned. He walked toward the animal.

"Here, kitty, kitty, kitty. Nice kitty."

Hiss.

"Don't, Skippy," she squealed, and wiggled away from his tickling hands.

"Lay still," he hissed.

"Noooo." The "o" ended in an uplift, a particular trait of her lilting accent.

"*Si.*"

She giggled again as his hands probed.

"Skippy," she complained, "don't. I'm sore."

"C'mon."

They both laughed and rolled in the bed, their arms tightly wrapped around each other. Their clothes lay scattered around the room, and the bedspread was rumpled under them.

"I love you," the boy said.

"You say that to all the girls." She pouted, her wide lower lip protruding. He nibbled on it.

"No, I don't," he protested.

"Yes, you do."

"No, I don't."

"Yes. *Si,* oooh, urn," she breathed, "do that again, Skippy."

His hand continued its probing at the junction of her silken thighs. She wiggled her bare buttocks, and he pinched the dark skin.

"Hey!"

"There's so much to grab hold of." He grinned.

She pouted again, and his mouth wandered from hers, down her neck and sternum to attach itself eagerly to one young breast.

"Oooh," she said again. "More. More."

He continued kneading her and licking and stroking, and she lay with her eyes closed. Suddenly her eyes flew open. She blinked.

"What was that?"

He raised his head from her breasts. He looked around and cocked his head. "Nothing, Maria."

"No. Listen." She grabbed at his exploring hand and held it.

There was a sound of crunching outside.

"Maybe it's old Epimenio with his wheelbarrow," Skippy suggested. He grinned.

"Oh, sure. Epimenio never hissed," the black-haired girl said.

"What?"

He cocked his head again, and sure enough, he heard it too.

Hiss. Hiss.

There was a bump against the outside adobe wall. "What was that?" Maria whispered to the boy. "It can't be my mother. She won't come back till late."

"I don't—"

The wall bulged. It fell in, with dried mud flying all over the small bedroom. The crucifix shot across the room, to land behind a wooden bench. Maria looked back over her bare shoulder as she struggled to unwind herself from the sheets. She screamed.

Large yellow eyes, evil in their intensity, stared down at her and the boy.

Hiss. Hiss.

She screamed again.

"Jesus Christ," Skippy moaned as he threw himself off the bed. His foot caught in the hand-dyed bedspread and he landed on the floor. He shrieked over and over as giant jaws closed about his torso, snapping him in the middle as if his body were a twig.

Maria watched in mute horror as the creature raised its head, Skippy's arms flailing. She watched the blood drip from the nightmare's jaw, heard the crunch of teeth against bone. Bits of warm wet flesh slipped from the mouth, dripping down on the bed and on the girl, who was frozen to the spot. An overwhelming rotting odor flooded the room and she gagged, one small hand to her nose and mouth.

Maria tried to cry, but there were no tears. She began to pray as the orange-and-black creature opened its mouth, what remained of Skippy's body sliding out. The nightmare reached for her.

"Who've y'all been with now?" Adele Foster demanded harshly. She rubbed a hand across her forehead and stared at her husband, who stood, his shirttail hanging out, the laces of his shoes untied.

"Nobody," Mike Foster muttered. He sniffed, then belched.

"Y'all been drinkin'," she accused. She looked at his sweating face, the red in his eyes.

"No law," Mike slurred.

Adele tapped an impatient foot. "Y'all've been out with that cheap Mexican whore again."

He ducked his head and mumbled. "No."

"Ah know y'all have. Don't go and deny it." She turned her back on him and began searching through the kitchen cabinets, as if seeking something to do, something on which to take out the anger.

"Bitch." It was said in, a low tone that she recognized.

"Don't start callin' me names," Adele warned.

"Fucking bitch," her husband said.

"Sit down," she said, whirling and pushing his chest. His knees gave out and he fell back onto the straight-backed plastic chair with its torn seat that had been crudely mended with cellophane tape.

A cockroach scuttled in one of the cabinets as she swung the door open.

"Damned bugs," she muttered, swatting at it with her hand and missing.

"Got bigger ones in Texas, don't you, bitch?"

She ignored him and went over to the white stove, stained through the years. She turned on the front burner, setting the coffeepot on it.

"Y'all sober up soon enough. Ah don't want the kids seein' y'all like this."

He belched for an answer, and she whirled on him, struck him, her palm flat out. The slap knocked his head to the side, and momentarily his watery blue eyes crossed from the unexpected blow. Then he was on his feet, twisting her arm up high behind her back.

"Goddammit!" Mike yelled in her face, and she turned her head away, smelling the stale alcohol, the musky odor of another woman's body on his breath.

"Let go, you disgustin' bastard," she yelled.

"Dropping your accent now, aren't you, bitch? No! I'm not going to let you go!"

"I hate you!"

"You frigid bitch! It's no wonder I go to Juanita when you're so cold—"

"Cold? Cold! And Ah gave y'all six kids—"

"Kids don't mean a fuckin' thing!"

"Mommy!"

He let her go, and she turned, her chest heaving, her face flushed. "What?"

The little boy stood in the doorway, one thumb implanted in his mouth. In the other hand was an eyeless teddy bear. The boy's footed sleepers were worn and patched in places.

"Mommy," he repeated, his big brown eyes large at having seen his parents hit each other.

"Yes?" She went to him.

"Davey scared."

"Davey doesn't have to be scared," Adele said. "Big bug outside."

"You and your goddamned New Mexico," she shot over her shoulder to her husband, who stood staring at his son. "Just had to come here."

"Beats workin' in the fields in Texas."

She muttered something under her breath that he didn't catch.

"Mommy."

It was a second child, Jane. Her blue eyes were wide with fear, and she was trembling.

"I heard a noise outside, Mommy."

"There are always noises outside," her mother said irritably. "Go back to bed, all of ya. It's late."

"No," Jane said, her face serious. "There's something—"

A shriek sounded from the back of the house and there was a crash, as if a wall had been struck. There were more screams and whimpers.

Adele ran down the narrow, barely lit hallway. Behind her stumbled the drunken Mike. She stopped at the door of one room.

"Oh, my God. Oh, my God," she repeated over and over.

"What is it?" her husband asked. He pushed his way past her and stared, sobering quickly.

The wall of the house *had* been pushed, and immense yellow eyes, six pairs of them, stared in at the house's occupants. Blood had spattered the carpet, the dingy walls, the three narrow beds in the room. The three older children were nowhere to be seen.

"Lizards," Mike said, his mouth hanging open.

"Where's the baby?" Adele asked the little girl. Her mind was numb; she could barely think. This wasn't real. It couldn't be.

Jane pointed toward her parents' room.

"Get the baby."

The little girl started toward the master bedroom, when one of the walls bulged and fell in, and more yellow eyes stared in. She shrieked and fled to her mother.

"Daddy, Daddy, what is them?" asked Davey.

Mike Foster could only stare.

The lizard pushed past the remnants of the wall, stepped on narrow twin beds as if they were matches, and advanced on the four remaining members of the Foster family.

He saddled the horse, cinched it tight, then turned to look at the townspeople gathered around him.

"I guess we'll be seein' you again, Sheriff," one of the men, a grizzled old-timer dressed in a Civil War uniform, said, breaking the silence.

He gazed at each one carefully, then spat in the earth. He pulled the gold star off his chest and tossed it down.

"Don't count on it," he said in a low voice.

Swinging up into the saddle, he pulled the bay around and rode through the town's one street. The sunlight glinted off his blond hair, and his back was as ramrod-straight as they had ever seen it.

He rode on and on, until at last his figure and his horse were just a speck in the distance to the townspeople.

Leland Hauserbusch, a.k.a. Lee Houston, typed the words "The End," then paused, turned off his electric, typewriter, and leaned back in his chair.

Another Captain Almozzo novel finished.

Hauserbusch rose, stretched, and padded over to the window. Eleven-thirty at night and he'd finally finished the fourth adventure of the Italian mercenary in the Southwest.

Yawning, he scratched his side. Maybe he would go to bed. It was still early for him, but he had worked straight through for the past forty hours, and he did deserve a break, after all.

70

Well, his editor had better be happy with this novel. He liked it, and God knows he didn't like very many of the books he'd written over his thirty-year career.

He turned back, surveying the room, bookshelves from floor to ceiling on two long walls. He gazed at ten shelves—those were for his own books.

Thunder Across the Arroyo. River Cowboy. Ride to the Rio. And all the others, dozens and dozens of them, that had made him America's best-known Western writer since Zane Grey.

Hauserbusch lit a cigarette, coughed, then paced out to the kitchen to get a drink. Booze and cigarettes. *What a cliché for a writer*, he thought with a wry smile. He glanced out the window as he poured the whiskey and noticed the flickering lights in the distance.

Probably something on the plaza. Teenagers. His upper lip curled in disgust. He hated teenagers. He hated, most particularly, the teenagers of this town, who seemed to delight in tormenting him in some way or another. They knew he had to be left alone. They knew he didn't like visitors or interruptions. And yet they would phone him at strange hours and then hang up when he answered; they would ring the doorbell and scuttle off into the desert before he could open the door.

Damned little bastards, he thought to himself. He polished off the shot of whiskey, then headed back to his study.

Yellow lights now. The son of bitches were no doubt building fires.

He opened the window and yelled, "Hey! Stop that! Don't you know there's a law against starting fires around here?"

But no one answered. He thought he heard faint cries and screams, but it was hard to tell over the sound of the wind.

The yellow came closer, and Leland Hauserbusch stared. It was a large eye … no, two eyes, and they were looking at him.

Panicked, the writer turned, running from the room. He ran from the house. He wanted to get away from what he had seen looking in at him. But they were all around.

Large lizards that crawled through the sand and the desert and the town. Now that Hauserbusch was outside, he could hear the screams of agony. In the blaze of moonlight he saw what appeared to be the arms and legs of struggling humans in the mouths of the giant lizards.

Hot bile rose to his lips and spewed out onto the ground. Sweat popped out on his skin, despite the coolness of the wind, and his hands began to shake.

What could he do? Where could he go? Hauserbusch looked around wildly, but everywhere he looked, he saw the creatures.

They made no sound except a low *hiss, hiss, hiss.* It was almost as though millions of snakes were gathered to make that sound.

Leland bolted, seeking escape. There was a wide distance between the legs of two of the creatures. He would run through that. He would escape. He would never return to Lagarto. He would get the hell out of there.

He gave no thought to the townsfolk, to his neighbors. He ran.

He did not see the giant reptilian mouth weaving in the air, moving slowly toward him, the widening of the jaw, the sticky yellow-green ooze that dripped from the reptile's teeth.

He did not see this. Death was instantaneous when the teeth ground through his spine.

The giant reptiles crawled past Lagarto, leaving nothing alive in their wake. Long trails of blood and a yellowish, sticking ooze traced obscene patterns in the dirt and along the pavement.

Herds of cattle scattered before the assault of the Gilas, and the night air was filled with the plaintive cry of dying cattle.

Carl Cjeke lifted his head from the thinness of the bunk's pillow and blinked in the darkness. He heard the noise again. At first he had thought it was part of his dream, but now he realized it wasn't.

He rose, dressed in the darkness, left the small bunkhouse, and started toward the main house.

At the edge of the yard he could see something moving. The moon had momentarily gone behind a cloud, and nothing could be seen clearly. Above the wind he thought he heard a hissing sound.

The clouds scudded past, and the moon's light was once more unobstructed.

He blinked at what he saw.

Giant lizards … giant Gila monsters.

"Get up," he yelled, cupping his hands. He ran toward the house, pounded on the door.

A light went on, deep inside, and a window was thrown open. "What? Who's there?"

"It's me, Señor Baca. There' somethin' awful out here," Carl yelled. "Get out. Run for it!"

Cjeke heard a staccato burst of Spanish, then more lights were being turned on. He could hear the approach of the creatures.

Hiss. Hiss. Hiss.

He ran to the garage, threw open the door, jumped into the jeep, and backed it out. The creature, its large yellow eyes unblinking, was heading toward the house. It was followed by other lizards like it. Their heads touched the adobe walls, pushed, poked, and the dried mud crumbled.

There were screams and cries as the reptilian heads searched for members of the Baca family.

Sobbing, Cjeke pulled out his rifle and aimed at the nearest creature. The bullet impacted with a thud, but it did not slow the creature down, much less stop it. He pumped more bullets into the lizard, then reloaded. He fired and fired.

Nothing helped.

He couldn't hear anything from the Bacas. All he saw was a ruined house, and an arm, as if casually tossed away, lying on the dirt in front of the hacienda. Crying once more, the tears running down his sun-darkened face, he reversed the jeep hard and floorboarded it, heading toward Lagarto. He would warn the townsfolk, maybe have the army come out and shoot these big bastards.

Something had to be done.

He jounced and jolted over the rough terrain, weeping. The jeep sailed over a rise in the ground, the rise just five miles short of Lagarto, and he stopped the vehicle so abruptly it skidded.

There was no escape—not for him, not for the Bacas, not for Lagarto. For from the village came the giant hellish lizards, and beyond them, where the village should have been, there was rubble.

Cjeke wept, his hands covering his face.

Chapter 11

"Oh, brothers and sisters, I say unto you that at the end of your lives you face the damning hell-fires of everlasting perdition."

There was a moan spreading throughout the audience like the rustle of leaves in autumn. Someone cried out, "Save us, Jesus!"

The preacher, the well-fed Reverend J. W. Porter, paused in his harangue to survey the upturned faces spread out below him. He shook his head at their wickedness. He raised his fist and pointed with his forefinger to the sky, which was blocked by the immense yellow tent.

"Jesus will not save you," he bellowed.

There was the sound of weeping throughout the audience.

"You are doomed, brothers and sisters. Doomed." The word, amplified by the microphone, rolled through the tent like thunder. "Jesus will not help sinners like you!"

Some of his congregation fell onto their knees before their fold-up chairs and raised imploring hands toward Porter.

"Unless."

The one word hung there in the air, between the reverend and his weeping flock. They clung to it, sought that one word for the salvation they hoped would be theirs.

"Unless," Reverend Porter, a florid man with soulful eyes, continued, "you help yourselves."

"Amen, brother!"

"Jesus, Jesus, Jesus, save us!"

"Oh, help us, Jesus," a woman called out in the first row.

"'Help us, Jesus,'" the large preacher repeated, shaking his head. "Do you know what God says to you, brethren? He says help yourself first and then Jesus will help you. Help yourselves, brothers and sisters. Help yourselves!" He paused to take a drink of lemonade and licked his large fleshy lips. He mopped his sweating face with a rumpled white handkerchief.

"How do we help ourselves, Reverend?" a man in the back called out.

It was the question he was waiting for.

"It's not an easy road, brothers and sisters." His booming voice lowered a little. "No, it's not." Porter leaned back, his hands gripping the edges of the podium, and he stared out at them, those with their guilty consciences and those without. From time to time his stare would rest on an individual, who would feel the finger of shame creep up his or her spine.

"It's not an easy road," Reverend Porter repeated. "No, sir. But it can be done," his voice dropped, "if you have faith in Jesus."

"Oh, yeah," someone called.

"Amen!" several people cried fervently.

He sipped more lemonade. "But first … first you must learn something in order to be saved."

"Tell us, brother!"

"Jesus does not want to see all the earthly comfort you have laid up, at the risk of your immortal soul. No, He does not." He scowled at them.

"Tell us, tell us, tell us!" It became a chant, deadening all other noise, even the weeping.

"I'll tell you, brothers and sisters, how you can save your souls, how you can get forgiveness for our Lord Jesus Almighty." The

Reverend Porter dropped his hands below the podium and twisted a diamond ring embedded in the flesh of one pinkie.

"I'll tell you how," he said loudly. "Jesus—"

"Amen!"

He smiled. "Jesus does not care about your expensive clothes, or your newest car, or your promotion at the office. He doesn't. He cares about your *souls.* And He is concerned that all you, yes, you, brothers and sisters"—his sausage-like finger jabbed outward at the rapt people—"He is concerned that all of *you* do not care for your souls. Now, how does He want you to help yourselves? Why, brothers and sisters, it's not an easy road. No, sirree." Porter shook his head sadly. "But it is a *giving* road.

"Yes," he hissed, "Jesus wants you all to learn to give. To give of yourself, to give of your families, to give of your"—he paused, lowered his voice, so that the people listening to him had to lean forward to catch his words—"mammon. Give unto the Lord, and you will find the salvation for your wicked souls. Give of that unhealthy money that weighs you down to this clay earth. Give so that you might lighten your heart and soul. Give so that you will not burden yourself any further, and so that Jesus God Almighty can begin His wonderful healing of your sinful lives."

In the back of the large tent an organ, slightly tinny in tone, began playing an old hymn.

"Now, brothers and sisters, plates will be passed among you, and if you wish to purge yourselves of your sins, then give, give all that you can. The Lord does not care if it is merely a ten-dollar bill. The Lord amply wants you to cleanse your inner self. Now remember these words from the Holy Scriptures: 'God loveth a cheerful giver.' and 'Ye cannot serve God and mammon.'"

He paused, and the organ music swelled. The plates began passing down the rows of people, and there was the crumpling of many bills. The sea of green.

Over the sound of the organ the congregation could hear a hissing, as if air were escaping from a tire.

"You hear that?" Reverend Porter demanded. "Well, the Lord is weary unto death of your human pettiness and greed and miserly ways, and He has sent you adversity with which to wrestle."

More money was flung into the collection plates, so that the sea became a rain.

"Give of yourselves, give so that you might be clean and saved and born again," he exhorted them.

The back of the tent wobbled, and several people toward the rear screamed.

"The Devil! The Devil has come!"

Reverend Porter looked up from the sea of green and stared, his mouth agape.

Through the tent flap was thrust a large black-and-orange reptilian head, its hide like shiny beads. Its tongue, long and sinuous and evil-looking, flicked out, while its alien yellow eyes stared at the audience.

Reverend J. W. Porter moaned.

For a moment the reverend's audience was mesmerized by the sight of the lizard, then panic ensued.

"Now, brothers and sisters, let us pray to our Lord Jesus God Almighty," he called out, his voice booming.

But the sound of his admonition was lost in the screams and the cries of the running, stumbling people.

"Don't forget—get the money," The Reverend Porter screamed to his assistants as he abandoned the pulpit. He fell to his knees on the hard earth and began scrambling beneath the folding chairs, plucking up the larger denomination bills and thrusting them into his pockets.

The hissing grew louder, and now there was not one reptilian head staring in at them, but three.

Hiss. Hiss. Hiss.

"Give!" Reverend Porter shrieked, running in the opposite direction from the creatures from hell. He ran to get away from the Devil, away from the hell-spawn. In his hands were clutched green bills.

But it was too late. The large reptiles were easing their way inside, and unable to stand any longer, the tent began to collapse. Lights swung loose, people screamed, cried out as they trampled and were trampled, and the lizards kept coming until the canvas hit the earth.

The Gilas had brought the house down, and not even the sea of green could save those lost souls.

Chapter 12

"Ah gotta do *somethin'*," Governor Bubba J. Roy said emphatically. He brought a beefy fist down on the top of his desk so hard that his pens fell out of their holders. Sheepishly he replaced them. "Now, y'all unnerstand that?"

"Governor, Governor, please," said Hal Mondragon, spreading his hands in a conciliatory gesture. "You know that you have to do something; and I know that, too. But." He paused.

"Yeah?" Roy's pig eyes bored into him. "Yeah, but what? C'mon, boy, spit it out."

"Yes, sir." The lawyer smiled to himself. "There is a drawback to immediate action."

"Yeah?"

"Yes. And that is—if you act too quickly, *you might do the wrong thing.*"

"Wrong thing?" Bubba Roy echoed.

"Yes, sir."

"Wall, Ah wouldn't want that."

"No, sir."

"Might hurt me at the polls."

"Yes, sir."

"Might help my opponent."

"Probably would, sir."

Roy peered at Mondragon, who sat opposite him with a very interested, intense expression on his face. "What y'all suggest, Hal? Ah mean, after all, Ah gotta do somethin' right quick. Them *things* been eatin' people down south."

"Yes, sir. Voters, sir."

"That's right." Bubba sat back in his chair, which creaked ominously under his bulk. "Wall?"

"I think, Governor, that you should wait … and see what develops down in Otero County. You can always say you were studying the situation—which, of course," he hastened to add, "you are. I think the state could be harmed by something rash."

"Ah'll call in the marines. Them boys'll take care of them things."

"Eventually, sir. If you wait … long enough … there is the possibility of … federal aid."

"Federal aid?"

"Yes, sir. And then the state wouldn't have to pay for any relief. That would help the voters."

"Why, yes, it would." Bubba smiled to himself, a self-satisfied expression, as if he had come up with the solution himself. He frowned suddenly. "Ah sent that there girl down there. That Miz Dwah'yer."

"Yes, sir."

"What'll we do 'bout her?"

"Nothing, sir. I'm sure she can't be of much use. After all, she is an academician," Mondragon said smoothly.

"That's true enough, Ah reckon."

"And sir …"

"Yeah?"

"Perhaps in the next day or so, you can visit the stricken areas, make a tour of them, offer comforting words and—"

No further words were needed between the two men as they looked at each other and smiled.

81

And get votes.

"Ah got ya'll, son, loud and clear." Bubba grinned.

In the morning light the carnage looked worse than the mind could ever have imagined, Kate decided as the helicopter took a swing over the little town of Lagarto, or what remained of it.

What just twenty-four hours ago had been a sleepy village of some five hundred souls was no more.

Buildings lay in ruins, the adobe bricks tumbled carelessly, strewn as if by the child of some giant. Fences were crushed, livestock dead. Telephone poles and wires crisscrossed the dirt and dangled forlornly in the gray dawn.

Here and there, as the copter made its sweep, she and Chato could see the brown of an arm, a leg, sometimes two eyes staring up out of a half-eaten, half-crushed head.

Nausea gnawed at her stomach, clawed its way to her throat, and threatened to spill out. She gulped rapidly, in an effort to keep the bile down. Glancing at Chato, Kate saw that his face was pale. Their hands met, gripped as they surveyed the destruction.

The helicopter's pilot, on loan from the military, seemed to relish what he saw, or the scientist decided, he was merely exhibiting a ghoulish curiosity. His eyes, behind the mirrored Air Force sunglasses, could not be seen.

Lower and lower the copter spiraled. Chato pointed soundlessly and Kate nodded.

Most of the corpses they saw were cut in half at the waist.

"Gilas chew in a sideways motion," she supplied, half-whispering to herself.

"What?" Chato yelled over the noise of the chopper blades.

She repeated what she had said, and watched as more color drained from his face.

Around the victims and their appendages stood pools of a greenish-yellow liquid. The pilot set the copter down, and Kate got out to investigate.

She pressed a handkerchief to her nose and mouth, for, though the sun was still low in the sky, the day threatened to be very hot. Already the flesh of the dead was beginning to swell and turn black. Maggots crawled across the heads of little children, the hands of mothers.

Kneeling, she put a finger out and felt the viscosity of the liquid in one of the pools. She smelled it. There was no doubt.

The venom of the Gila monster.

Yet, as she looked around, Kate thought that the victims probably had not been killed by the poison at all. They had been chewed to death. She shuddered.

Walking past a small wheelbarrow, its faded sides now stained a rusty color from blood, she returned to the helicopter. She nodded to the pilot, and he took the copter up.

"Fly over the Sands," Kate yelled.

The pilot nodded.

"What do you think you'll see?" Chato called over the sound of the engine and the blades.

The woman shook her head, then twisted a red curl around one finger as she looked out at the landscape rushing under them. "Don't know. Maybe we'll see something. Anything, I guess. Perhaps a burrow." But she really doubted it—not now, not with the sun up. The only incident with Gilas in the day had been on a cloudy morning, very early, and she did not think that would happen again. Why, she couldn't say, but she just felt it.

The swing over White Sands proved futile. Pass after pass over the gypsum sand revealed not a sign of the Gila monsters.

Watching his face, Kate wondered if Chato were thinking of his university days when he had lectured about White Sands, of the times he had organized field trips to the national monument. He looked up and his black eyes met her blue ones, and he smiled, touching her cheek gently with his hand.

"That's odd," she called, after the pilot glanced back at her. "They're cold-blooded and so they should be more active during the warm hours of the day, and sluggish at night."

"That's right," Chato said, "yet all the attacks have been at night."

"Maybe they're mutants," the pilot suggested.

Kate nodded. "I'd like to find their burrow," she said.

"What do you want me to do now?" yelled the pilot.

"Return us to Tones, please. We won't find the burrows today."

Within fifteen minutes they were once more in the small town. After some discussion with Chato, Kate had decided to maintain her "headquarters" in the town, as it was close to White Sands, which had seen the beginning of the Gila activity, and she wanted to remain in one spot in case the governor contacted her.

"Call the governor," Chato suggested as they walked, hand in hand, back to the Golden Palomino Motel. Kate was aware that the townspeople were staring at the Indian man and Anglo woman walking together, being, she almost chuckled, *intimate*.

"And what then?" Kate asked.

"Well, we don't know how many of the buggers there are, and we don't know where their burrows are. Seems to me that the governor should have one of the military branches send some choppers out with infrared equipment."

"That seems logical enough," the woman said.

"Only Bubba hasn't done it."

"At least that we know of," she said.

"You know," Chato said with a slight smile, "I think you're apologizing for Bubba J. Roy."

Her indignant expression was answer enough, and he chuckled out loud.

They returned to the motel room, where Chato sat down at the dresser while Kate went over to the phone. She returned in a few minutes, a scowl on her face.

"They're not taking phone calls right now. They'll get back to us," she said angrily.

"Umm," he replied absently.

"Did you hear me?" she asked.

He looked up, meeting her eyes in the mirror. "I did now," he said with a smile. "What's the matter?"

"The governor is 'out' presently and will return my call."

"Sounds like he's avoiding you," Chato said.

"Sounds that way to me, too."

He turned back to a large piece of paper in front of him and continued studying it. Corning up behind him, she massaged the muscles of his neck and shoulders.

"That feels so good," he said, leaning his head back against her. She smiled at him in the mirror and winked.

"I'll continue only if you do the same for me," Kate said.

"Gladly."

"It's so frustrating," she said.

"This situation with the governor?"

"That's right. *I* can't do anything; I'm only a private citizen. You and I together can't even do anything—besides making nuisances of ourselves. Doesn't he realize that people are being killed down here?" she demanded, grinding the heel of her hand into Chato's shoulder.

"Ouch! Watch it! That's me you're abusing."

"Sorry."

"Well, effectively our hands are tied," Chato said, his eyes half-closed. "And these Gilas keep going on a rampage. I wonder," he paused, "I wonder what made them act up at this particular time."

"Maybe because it's getting cooler now," the woman suggested. "The really hot days of summer are over."

"Yeah ... maybe. Except that it's been warm, really warm, every day—or night—they've attacked." He pushed some hair off his forehead. "Why would these normally gentle animals go berserk and start rending humans limb from limb?"

"Well, now that they're giants, we might just seem to be little rodents ... their normal prey," Kate said.

"Yeah."

"And also we really don't know what that dose of radiation back in 1945 did to them. Could have made them very different from the Gilas we're accustomed to."

"Good point," Chato said, a slight smile on his face. She leaned over and kissed his ear. "I like that part of the massage."

"It's your turn to rub," she whispered.

He sighed. "I knew it was too good to continue indefinitely."

They exchanged places and she stared down at the map he had been studying. His hands, with their blunt strong fingers, caressed her neck, rubbed her shoulders.

"Take off your blouse," Chato ordered.

She unbuttoned the gray blouse, let the silky material slide to her waist, then leaned back as his fingers deftly undid the catches of her bra. He tossed the bra away and then began to work his fingers through the sore and tense muscles.

"What were you looking at?" she asked him, indicating the map. "Why the sudden interest?"

From the action of his hands on her back, her breasts bobbled slightly, loosened as they were from the confines of the lacy brassiere. She smiled, looked in the mirror and caught his eye on them, and sat up straighter. Reaching down, he tweaked one rosy nipple.

"Ummm, good," she said, "but you haven't answered my question."

"Well, study the map for a moment," Chato said. "The red circles are sites of the Gila attacks."

Kate's eyes swept over the map of New Mexico. "Yes," she said slowly. "There's the arroyo where the school bus crashed; the diner outside the White Sands Monument; Lagarto."

His massage was easing her, and she was drifting off. She tried to keep her eyes open, but it seemed impossible. The cold air of the air-conditioned room had stiffened her nipples, and she felt oddly vulnerable without her blouse. Yet she was so comfortable she didn't want to move to put it on again.

Suddenly the back rub stopped and she felt the warmth of Chato's hands as he cupped each breast. "Nice," she murmured. He pinched her nipples, hard, and her eyes flew open.

"Chato!"

"Wanted to get your attention again," he said, grinning.

"Red devil," she grumbled affectionately as she rubbed her outraged nipples.

"Now," he said, taking the stance of a teacher before a class, "geologists are good at two things. One: they can read maps like hell. Two: they taste rocks."

"What?" she asked, startled.

"Yes, indeed, they taste rocks."

"Well, there are no rocks here to lick." She felt, rather than saw, the leer.

"Oh, I don't know about that," he said casually. "Chato. Business. Remember?"

"Oh, yeah. Business. Damn. Well, back to the drawing board, or more precisely, the map. I'm more attuned to maps than most people." He peered at her in the mirror. "Do you see a pattern?"

She stared at it again and frowned. "Oh, my God," she whispered.

"As far as I can tell," Chato announced, "the lizards are leaving the southern part of the state. They're heading north, and at the direction they're taking, they'll soon reach Albuquerque."

"And a third of the state's population is there," Kate said. "What do we do?"

"Call the Governor, I suppose."

She started to rise.

"But not now," he said. "That old shit-kicker won't be available to talk to you. Wait until later. Besides," he offered, "you know, it's not only your nipples that are erect."

Kate glanced at his crotch and laughed. "What do you suggest?"

He told her.

And they did.

Chapter 13

Fairtime.

An annual event, the fair was always eagerly anticipated by the residents of Sierra County, and especially in Cotton Springs, where it was held year after year. It was the residents' sole opportunity to do themselves up proud, to show off Cotton Springs, and to bring in more revenue to a sleepy little desert town that was located between Alamogordo and Socorro, and was the proverbial backside of nowhere.

Agricultural exhibits, handicrafts, jewelry-making, horse shows, rides on the midway, tractor and farm-equipment displays, baking contests, and a concert by mariachis in the plaza had been going on since early in the morning, when the fairgrounds opened to the public, and all vied for equal attention from the fairgoers.

Now dusk was falling, and in the grayness of early evening the lights of the fair were beginning to come on, one by one.

White lights, like small stars, looped through the midway, showering it with a blazing light, casting harsh shadows on the dirt, giving a glare to the arcade that made it even uglier than in the day. Couples walked hand in hand, oblivious to the sharp reality of the midway.

"Come, gitcher sweetheart a bear," called one of the carny men, his white apron streaked with black.

"Come in, come in," another yelled, an unlit cigarette dangling from his mouth. "See the two-headed calf! It eats! It moves!"

"Over here, young ladies, come here and see the world's strongest man!"

"Here now, boys and girls, free bunnies and ducks to the lucky lad or lass who can toss five nickels onto the plate!"

"Win!"

"Try your luck!"

"C'mon!"

"Win!" came the tantalizing shouts.

Angel Carlos Montoya hobbled down the hard-packed dirt of the midway and looked around with a faint smile creasing his weathered face. *Loco doctors*, he thought. They had wanted to cut him up for some *estúpido* pain that came and went, like the Coyote in the henhouse. Here one moment, gone the next, but always to return. Still, he'd fooled the gringo doctors. He'd sneaked out of the hospital and come on foot to the fair.

Hadn't missed one fair in over eighty-seven years, had he? He didn't remember the early ones, of course, having been just a baby. But he'd gone in his mother's arms. He wouldn't miss this one either, not for a little pain.

Maybe it was too much corn. Always gave him gas. He'd have to lay off the corn tortillas for a while. Stick with the flour ones.

Fair ... it was different now. In the old days it had been simpler, slower than the ones today. Quiet, too. Now they had the Ferris wheels and the loop-the-mouse and the roller coaster and all the other noisy rides that appealed to the young kids. Everywhere you turned, too, you saw the concession stands filled with their junk food. Couldn't hardly find enchiladas, or tacos, or just plain chili.

But still, these fairs had their good moments, their fun places to visit. Like the animal barns, the stalls where they kept the show horses, the agricultural building, and of course, the building where they judged the pies, the cakes, the pickles, the preserves.

He remembered his mother faithfully entering her pickled chili into the fair each year. She'd won, too, and those judges, mostly gringos, with the puckered mouths and tears rolling down their cheeks, had been mute testimony to the goodness of that chili. Anna, too, had entered exhibits. Mostly decorated cakes. But that had been before her death nearly six years ago.

Angel sighed and paused, lifting a bottle of wine wrapped in a paper sack, the rim of it just sticking above the brown paper. He didn't care for wine, didn't approve of it. But this was different. This was medicinal. It helped take away some of the pain, the pain inside his body, the pain in his mind when he thought of Anna and their years together. And, without the pain coursing through his body, he could come to the fair and have fun. Like in the old days.

Putting the bottle to his lips, he tilted his head back and swallowed mouthful after mouthful of the red liquid. A thin red line trickled down his chin. He choked a little, then wiped his mouth on the back of his brown hand. Angel Montoya stared across the tops of the tents of the midway at the gray glimmer in the west and his band froze halfway down to his side.

"Madre de Dios!" he whispered hoarsely, and stared at the giant reptilian heads that loomed over the tents.

Julia Fremont leaned back against the hard wooden back of the bench and sighed. She ran her hands down the legs of her faded denims, then twisted a strand of gray-streaked russet hair behind her ear. She closed her eyes momentarily, then began ticking off the locations of the children on her fingers of the hand still resting on her jeans.

Karen would be in the baby animal barn, oohing and aahing at the chicks, the piglets, the tiny pony, and the goslings. Nate would be in the agricultural building, intently studying the various vegetables grown by the county's farmers, and his twelve-year-old face would be so serious. Anne would be in the horse arena, watching the hourly shows, reading her program book avidly and with equal eagerness studying the points of each mount. And as for the twins, well, she smiled fondly, Todd and Tony would be hand-in-hand on the midway strip, staring wide-eyed and openmouthed at the hawkers who'd bid them come and see the fattest woman in the world, the skinniest man, the Siamese twins, the rubber boy.

Julia glanced up at the darkening sky and touched the base of her throat, feeling the droplets of perspiration in the hollow there. It was so hot for this time of year. She studied the sky. Red streaks, tinged with gray and salmon and saffron, painted the sky with a typical lovely New Mexico sunset. She thought it was probably one of the reasons Ty had given up a perfectly good job in Ohio to move to New Mexico. He loved watching the sunsets. They'd moved, not to Albuquerque, nor to Santa Fe, but to Cotton Springs. Ty was a would-be farmer. No, more than that, for the farm had prospered in the past ten years. They weren't rich, but they were comfortable, and the kids rarely lacked anything.

She liked it here, no matter what she told him in the heat of an argument. She didn't miss Ohio, its weekend rains that spoiled their plans or the moisture-laden air that clogged your chest. She didn't regret moving away from family and friends to come to a little town in the middle of the desert, where half the residents didn't know English and the other half did little better.

She didn't.

She didn't even mind the alienlike plants and animals, so different from the familiar ones of the midlands.

Julia closed her eyes and breathed deeply, smelling the corn on the cob, the horse manure, the fragrant straw and hay, the sizzling hotdogs, and the dry smell of dust. You didn't have odors like these in the city, where the acrid pollution dulled your senses.

Probably should start to round up the kids, Julia thought. They'd have to be going pretty soon or Ty would get worried. He didn't like them out late at night, even shortly after nightfall, and it was a long way to the farm. She smiled to herself. He didn't realize that the desert wasn't like the city; it didn't hide criminals who could leap out at you from alleyways and bushes. The desert was harsh and hard, but it was far more honest.

But she could delay a few minutes more and let the kids enjoy themselves. After all, the fair came only once a year.

Her eyes still closed, she listened to the sounds of children screaming with delight on the raucous rides, of the animal sounds—bleating, neighing, lowing—and in the distance a faint sound she could not quite make out. She frowned, one ear cocked.

Hissing.

Startled, Julia opened her eyes and looked around, then gasped. Thickset giant lizards, their orange-and-black-banded hides, crawled on fat legs down the main street of the fairgrounds. The rounded muzzles and flattened heads swung from side to side, while yellow eyes glared malevolently in the gloom. The tails, fat and blunt and heavy, dragged behind the mammoth creatures, leaving a trench of crushed dirt and grass. Greenish-yellow ooze dripped from the open mouths, mouths filled with deadly sharp teeth. And there was the stench of calamus.

Gila monsters, Julia knew, and her heart began hammering. A cold finger of fear traced her spine and her legs trembled, threatening to buckle under her.

Long sinuous tongues flickered out, touching trees, people. Men and women screamed and raced from the path of death. An old Chicano fell down in his flight and was trapped by five-clawed feet. The creature's head reached down and picked up the man, whose screams of agony pierced Julia's skull. The lizard chewed sideways and the man's body slowly disappeared, as gobbets of wet flesh dripped unnoticed from the reptile's mouth. Blood seeped down the creature's chest, staining the beady hide red. The dirt beneath the reptile was crimson and wet.

Julia looked frantically back and forth, panic fighting with reason. Which child should she go after?

Her mind was made up for her when a familiar voice called to her. "Mom! Mom! Look at those lizards!"

It was Nate, and he stood just outside the agricultural building, staring up with morbid fascination at the approaching orange-and-black nightmares. The boy seemed rooted to the ground.

"Nate," the woman screamed. "Run! Come to me, Nate!"

But the child remained planted. She started running toward her son. A head, four or five feet across, broad with beaded hide, swayed, then dipped down toward the young boy. The mouth opened, revealing the awesome teeth inside, the teeth still covered with torn flesh. The forked tongue flicked out, obscenely stained with blood.

She stumbled toward him, fell, got up. "Nate," Julia cried, tears running down her face. She had to get to him. Rescue him. Grab him in her arms, run away with him.

But it was too late, and the hot bile came to her throat, choking her, causing her to retch, as she watched the teeth close down on her son. He cried out to his mother in his fear and torment, and screamed, sounds that bored like hot irons into her brain. She dropped to her knees to pray, but no words came. Hypnotized, frozen, Julia could not take her eyes away. She saw the mangled body of her son fall from the lizard's mouth, saw that only half of it was there and that the upper part of the torso, the shoulders and the head, remained in the lizard's mouth. Blood dripped from the jaw that ground slowly side to side as it methodically chewed its victim. Bones crunched with sickening regularity, and the greenish stickiness, now tinged with red, continued drooling from the creature's mouth.

She saw this, unfeeling, got to her feet, and slowly walked forward.

Sister Maria Rosario of Santa Cruz Convent in the Desert paused, her two little charges from the orphanage tightly grasping her hand. Today was a free day for her, and she had volunteered to take two orphans to the fair, an opportunity they would normally have missed.

They were filled with questions and enthusiasm, and continually pointed to this and to that—in fact, to anything they saw.

"Sister, Sister," said Teresa, pulling at the nun's hand. "What's that?" She pointed with her free left hand.

The nun looked up, then stared with mounting horror. "Dear Mother in heaven," she whispered, looking at the black-and-orange heads of the lizards that could be seen beyond the wooden palisade separating the game arcade and midway from the rest of the fair. Shooting up between the gruesome creatures were long fingers of yellow flames.

She turned to run with her two charges, but the black-and-orange reptiles were all around them. Advancing on her. Yellowish-green venom splashed to the ground from the tooth-filled jaws, and chunks of flesh fell from their mouths. The pathway behind them was smeared with blood, a grotesque and cruel mockery of a red carpet.

Dropping to her knees, the nun numbly fingered her rosary, her hands trembling.

"Pray, children."

"Why, Sister?" asked Juanita.

"Never mind, child. Pray with me." She forced her voice to remain calm, not to show the panic, the horror, the fear, the dread that welled up inside her. For there was no escape from these creatures, these demons of hell.

Her lips formed the words out of habit, and never had they been so heartfelt. "Hail Mary, full of grace ..."

Slowly the children fell to their knees and followed the nun in prayer. "... Now and in the hour of our deaths ..."

The lizards advanced.

Hunter Smith smiled at his son and clapped him on the shoulder. "First place, boy. That's real good."

Words of praise did not come easily from this man. Young Robin, towheaded and snub-nosed, flushed with pride. He scuffed his feet in the straw of the barn, thrust his hands deeper into his jeans' pockets, then looked up at his prize-winning Black Angus bull yearling and smiled.

He patted the bull's neck. It had paid off. All those long hours after school, and in the early dark hours of morning, and on weekends, missed vacations and parties and fun because of Willy here. But it didn't matter. Not now. Because Dad had said "good."

The bull moved, distinctly uneasy. His eyes rolled in his head, and the boy reassuringly patted his soft neck.

The older man raised his head and looked around. "What's all that commotion outside?" He sauntered over to the doorway and stared out. The color drained from Hunter's face.

"My God," he whispered. Then he ran back to his waiting son. "C'mon." He grabbed Robin's hand.

"What is it?" the boy asked.

"Never mind," Hunter Smith said harshly, "just c'mon." He pulled the boy away from the bull's pen.

"Dad, no, no," Robin yelled. "I can't leave Willy!"

"Come on!" his father thundered, and jerked Robin's arm. Picking the boy up, he ran toward the door opposite the one he had looked out.

But it was too late.

Orange-and-black clawed feet appeared in the door. The wall bulged in, then crumbled as the huge reptile crawled into the livestock barn. It moved its head from side to side, and the man and boy could hear muffled screaming, as though coming from the reptile's mouth.

Blood spurted from its jaws, soaking the straw and dirt floor. Abruptly the noise stopped.

Robin shrieked and struggled in his father's arms. Tears coursing down his lean face, Hunter looked from one side of the barn to the other. There had to be another way out. There just had to be.

He put his son down and held out his hand. "Robin, we've got to make a run for it. Are you game?"

The boy gazed solemnly up at his father's face, so pinched and frightened and alien. Mutely he nodded. Then he turned once to stare at Willy.

Panicked at the sight of the hissing lizards, the bull was tugging at the rope drawn through its nose ring. It jerked its head from one side to another, seeking escape.

"I gotta let Willy go," the boy cried, running back toward the Angus bull.

"No, Robin! No," his father shouted. The man Watched as the boy slipped the loop of rope off the post and patted the heaving sides of the bull. The animal lowered its head.

"No," Hunter Smith screamed, racing toward his son. He flung Robin out of the way just as the bull charged. Up over the bull's head, his side sliced open, blood spraying over the bull and the boy, the tall man was tossed in an obscene parody of the ancient Minoan bull dance. Down he fell onto the hard dirt of the floor, and he felt the crack of his spine, the pain invade his body. Something wet touched his outflung hand and he realized, with a distant feeling, that it was his own blood seeping into the dirt and the straw.

Far, far away he could hear a screaming, and he realized it was his son. He tried to look over at Robin to reassure him, but he could not move his head. He tried to speak, but no words came.

Slowly a red mist began to envelop his eyes, and a long, obscenely long, object flickered into his range of vision.

Hiss. Hiss.

He saw orange and black, felt the tongue wrap itself around his lower body. He felt the forked tongue pulling him toward the mouth filled with the sharp teeth. The sharp teeth that oozed the nauseating green venom.

As the teeth closed about his waist, severing the bones, causing them to splinter, bringing even more pain than the bull's goring, Hunter Smith found his voice to scream.

Onward the giant Gila monsters came, each footstep they took bringing death and destruction.

One reptile brushed against the brightly lit Ferris wheel. The riders screamed in terror and panic, and some jumped, preferring to end their lives that way, quickly, while others still clung tenaciously to life.

A little girl, with blue ribbons in her long blonde hair, teetered, the gondola in which she rode swinging back and forth as though from a strong wind. She clung desperately to the roll bar as the cage front opened. Then the bar gave way, flinging her outward. She fell with a shrill cry.

The Gila monster reached its massive head down and began chewing on the bodies at its feet, pawing through them as though searching for a choice morsel. Legs, arms, and torsos disappeared into the cavernous maw. Disjointed bones, flesh still clinging to them, were scattered. When it was finished with its meal, the lizard crawled on, the weight of its body and fat tail pushing corpses fiat into the ground. Some flesh adhered to the beady skin and was dragged along, becoming coated with bloody mud.

Around the around the merry-go-round whirled, the gaily painted horses and giraffes and swans twirling in a gaudy blur of color. The music tinkled tinnily, and the children shrieked with delight.

They shrieked again as the giant orange-and-black lizards approached, the forked tongues flicking out. Adults ran past them, their eyes unseeing, some running into the electrical cables of the amusement rides.

The adults fell down and didn't move, even as showers of sparks covered them. Some got to their feet, hands bloody, clothes torn, and continued to run.

The lizards reached the merry-go-round and the children, afraid of the lizards, of the strange adults, tried to get off their painted wooden mounts. But the operator was no longer there. He had run away, leaving the children to fend for themselves.

The merry-go-round continued to whirl, and as a child fell off, hitting the switch that controlled the speed, the ride increased in speed. Some of the children were flung far away from the ride, their little bodies crashing into the sides of tents, of concession booths, onto the ground, where they were trampled by the unseeing adults. Others clung to their horses and giraffes and swans, and cried out as they watched the lizards' mouths open.

The Ferris wheel toppled, crashing into the tent where the fattest woman alive was exhibited. Electrical sparks flew in every direction, and the sparks caught on the canvas of the tent. Some fell on the clothing of the panic-stricken people. Soon a fire was blazing, and it leaped from tent to tent, from tent to dry wooden arcade. Over the roaring of the fire could be heard the continual screaming of the panicked and dying humans, the crying of children, the hissing of the lizards.

Smelling the acrid odor of smoke and fear, the horses kicked at their stalls and plunged in the narrow wooden confines, seeking escape. Seeing no other alternative, Ben Chavez opened the doors. The horses thundered past him, in a flurry of moving legs, tails, and manes.

He watched sadly as they disappeared beyond the stalls, and thought of the lost money and time. But it didn't matter any longer. Not really. Not in the face of death.

He sat down on a crate, his legs stretched out in front of him, his hands folded. He watched the flies buzz around a fresh pile of manure.

And he thought of the show horses that he might have trained, had things been different.

And he waited for the reptiles.

Death and destruction reigned at the fair. The buildings were destroyed one by one as the lizards, seemingly impervious to the barriers of walls and roofs, crashed into the flimsy structures. Fires ranged over the midway, spreading to other parts of the fairgrounds. Electrical lights flickered as the power surged, wavered, blinked, then went off. Screams of trapped animals and humans alike could be heard in the relative coolness of the early evening. Crunching and hissing and shrieking were the dominant sounds.

Blood ran like a river through the animal barns, the midway, the main street. Half-eaten legs, arms, some hands still clutching papers and snow cones, were casually tossed aside. Heads stared sightlessly up at the sky, expressions of horror fixed on them for all time. Bits of flesh clung to the cottonwood trees that graced the fairgrounds, and above all could be heard the hissing.

When darkness fell totally, all that could be heard was the crackling of the fires, and a few faint screams, and the terrified weeping of a tiny girl in a bloodstained yellow-and-white dress, who stumbled aimlessly.

The fires flickered against the black backdrop of the New Mexico sky, feeding on the wood, on the piles of bodies.

Fairtime.

Chapter 14

"Well, now, Miz Dwah'yer, Ah cain't believe them big ol' lizards could attack Albuquerque," the governor's voice said.

Kate frowned at the receiver and shook her head when Chato raised an inquiring eyebrow. "Governor Roy, look at your reports. The Gilas are moving northward. They *will* reach Albuquerque, unless something is done."

"Ah jes' dunno 'bout that, ma'am." She heard the rustle of papers, and his chair creaked audibly. He cleared his throat. "Wall now, Ah'm gonna have to git on back to y'all," he announced.

"Very well, Governor." Scowling, she replaced the receiver on the cradle. "Shit-kicker," she muttered under her breath.

"I didn't think a nice girl like you from back East knew words like that," Chato teased.

"I learn fast," she said with a half-smile.

"I'll say," he murmured as he nuzzled her shoulder. He grinned. "Come back to bed."

She leaned back against him and studied the plaster ceiling. Chato traced the line of her jaw with one finger.

"He's a fool," Kate said.

"He's a politician. It's basically the same thing."

"How many people will have to be killed before he does something?"

"Just the opposition," Chato joked.

"Be serious," she said, wiggling away from him. He shrugged and turned over onto his back, his hands locked behind his head.

The phone rang then, and in the momentary stillness of the room the two people jumped. Kate grabbed the receiver.

"Hello?"

"Miz Dwah'yer? This here's the guv'nor."

As if she couldn't tell from his voice, she thought wryly.

"Ah been thinkin' 'bout what y'all said, and Ah'm gonna contact the prez'dent. We got ourselves 'nother report. More people killed, jes' a few miles north of the last one. It's jes' terrible, jes' terrible." And for the briefest moment there was a tremulous note in his voice.

And she almost believed him. *Hoary old actor*, part of her said, and she turned her attention back to what he was saying.

"Keep in contact, will you?" she asked. "I need up-to-date reports as quickly as possible."

"Yes, ma'am, Ah sure 'nuff will, and tomorrow ... why, by tomorrow mornin' the gub'ment should be actin'."

They hung up, and Kate rolled over to Chato and kissed him.

"The governor?" he asked.

"The governor," she confirmed. "He's going to ask for federal aid. By tomorrow we should see something done—or so the man says." She smiled at him. "But until then we'd best occupy ourselves."

He grinned wolfishly. "A delightful prospect, my dear."

Early in the morning, before the sun was fully up, they left the Golden Palomino Motel and found that something had indeed been done. Overnight, Torres had been turned into a circus.

Someone, somewhere, had leaked the story of the giant Gila monsters to the news services.

Everywhere the couple looked in the small town they saw network reporters running back and forth with microphones and shoulder cameras and long snaking cables, and around them stood a deep circle of curious onlookers who'd wandered in from different points of the town. There were makeup people and directors and people with clipboards and bored-looking electricians.

Walking hand in hand down Torres' main street, the couple watched silently. The reporters, from both television and newspapers, were busily engaged in interviewing the bewildered townsfolk, some of whom replied in monosyllables. Others were taking full advantage of the opportunity.

"Is this *really* TV?" one old guy asked, peering into the camera.

"Hey, don't do that," the reporter shouted. He pushed back the townsman, who glared at him.

"What time is this going to be on?" someone asked. "Hey, me ... hey, me, man! I'm on here!" another yelled. "Lookit here, okay? I show you—"

"I seen them!" someone else thundered. "I'm an eyewitness!"

"Hey, Mike, get a camera shot of that old geek. Yeah, thanks."

Chato grinned at Kate, who smiled.

A man with a harried expression, large sweat stains spreading across his shirt, ran past, panting. "Is Dr. Dwyer around?" he called to one of his cohorts, who paused in the action of putting a mini-cam to his shoulder.

"*Who?*"

"Goddamn, Leo, that's the broad who started all this. Remember?"

"Oh, yeah. Don't know. Whyn't you ask some of the locals? They might know."

"I've gotta get an interview with her. New York is *demanding* ten seconds with her." He blinked quickly. "Those damned yokels don't know the bitch from a hole in the ground."

Chato and Kate exchanged looks. "I won't tell if you won't," she said.

He shook his head. "You don't need that kind of rap."

The first man dashed off, unaware of their words or presence.

They continued walking, playing a game of identifying the national television reporters. All three networks had sent some of their top people. The pace was frantic and tempers were short, with the result there was a great deal of shouting and obscenity.

"Somehow I didn't think they'd behave like this," Chato said. "Just thought they'd have more dignity or something like that."

"They're human, too. I guess," Kate remarked, and he winked at her. "How thrilling to be at the core of all this excitement," she said dryly as she watched three reporters almost come to blows over some minor squabble. "Maybe I'll get my face on the cover of *Time* magazine."

"No," Chato said with mock seriousness, "they'll probably put a Gila monster on it."

"Too true." She squinted, looking into the distance, then pointed. "What's that at the end of the street?"

He stared in the direction she indicated. "I don't know." He shrugged.

"Some Indian scout you'd have made. C'mon. It looks fairly intriguing."

Picking up their pace, Chato and Kate reached the end of the street, where they found a hastily constructed wooden booth, like the stands for the Fourth of July fireworks. Overhead, attached by strings, bobbed light-colored balloons. Paper streamers decorated the front of the booth. A large hand-lettered sign proclaimed: "GILAS ON SALE. CHEAP."

They surveyed the boothkeeper's wares: hastily made Plaster of Paris statues of Gila monsters, with orange-and-black paint applied in a layman's approximation of the lizard's unusual striae. There were also felt pennants attached to dowel pins with Gilas or them. They looked like high school football pennants.

"I'd like one of those," Kate said, pointing to small statue at the back.

"Five dollars," the old man said, grinning at her.

"Highway robbery," she said in an aside to Chato She gave the old man the bill and took the statue. The oldster's seamed face beamed his pleasure.

"What are you going to do with it?" Chato asked.

"Use it as a paperweight at the office, of course." She gazed at the figure in her hand. A crooked smile had been painted on the lizard's face so that it seemed to be leering. With a sigh she slipped it into her shoulder bag.

Suddenly a few yards away a large VW bus pulled to a halt with a screech of brakes, a flurry of squawking chickens, and out poured a group of college-age men and women, all identically dressed in T-shirts, faded blue jeans, and sandals. Large signs were unloaded, and round metal buttons appeared on the T-shirts. Kate moved closer to the group.

"'Save the Gilas,'" she read out loud. "'Gilas are a natural resource.' 'Stop the slaughter—save the Gilas.'" A stunned expression on her face, she glanced at Chato.

"Obviously they're a bit confused about who's slaughtering whom," he said.

"What group are you?" Kate asked one of the girl going by. Her long blonde hair was pulled back into ponytail, and she wore seven buttons on her cream-colored shirt.

"NOPE," the girl responded.

"I beg your pardon?"

"NOPE. The National Organization for the Preservation of Everything."

"Oh, *those* people," Kate said slowly.

"Yeah, last year we stopped the government pig from putting in a dam that would have damaged all the elm trees in the valley."

"And didn't the river flood because there wasn't a dam?" Kate asked.

"Act of God," the girl said with a shrug. "Actually we're a subgroup of NOPE. SOPS. Save Our Poor Species."

Under her breath, Kate said to Chato, "This is probably their task force—Help the Underprivileged Gila. HUG."

"*Loca*," Chato said, and followed after Kate. "I don't understand why they'd want to save these beasts."

"It's obvious," Kate said.

He looked at her inquiringly.

"They're the only ones of their kind."

Kate spent the remainder of the day poring over the reports that continued to flood her one-room headquarters at the Golden Palomino Motel. The sheriff had offered her the use of his office but she had graciously declined. Now the reporters had discovered where she was based, apparently having bribed someone at the sheriff's office, and at Kate's request Chato was fielding the journalists' questions.

"Is it true that these Gila monsters are larger than elephants?" one reporter called out.

"Well, the one eyewitness account we've had did mention lengths up to fifteen feet," Chato replied cautiously.

"Jeezus," someone breathed.

Several reporters turned tail and pounded for phones report this latest news. Chato could well imagine the headlines: "GIANT GILAS SAVAGE NM." "FIFTEEN-FOOT-LONG KILLER REPTILES VICTIMIZE NM," or "LIZARDS LEAVE PATH OF DESTRUCTION."

Bulbs flashed; there was a whir of cameras.

"What caused them to grow so big?" another reporter called.

Chato resisted the impulse to reply "Lots of sunshine and good fresh air." Instead he replied, "Dr. Dwyer is attempting to determine the cause at this time."

"Hey, how'd an Indian get caught up in this?"

"Yeah," a bodiless voice said. "You talk real good for an Indian."

Chato stiffened, his eyes narrowing as he searched the crowd for the heckler. Some of the newspeople had the grace to look embarrassed; others seemed to agree. He certainly wasn't winning any points as Kate's spokesman. Now he knew how presidential press secretaries felt.

"That's all I have for now, ladies and gentlemen" —there was a collective groan—"but as soon as we find out more, we'll let you know."

He turned and entered the motel room, locking the door behind him. He peered out through the curtain. Most of the newspeople still milled around. Someone pointed toward the window and he let the curtain fall.

"Damned scavengers," he muttered.

Kate, looking up from a report, pushed back strand of hair from her eyes. "Tough day with the barracudas?" she asked.

Chato nodded, but didn't elaborate. "What's the latest?"

Kate put down the sheaf of papers and stretched. "Nothing yet," she said, patting his hand. "The governor called a short time ago. He met with a group of concerned ranchers earlier today. They've flown in from the southern part of the state and are pretty damned irate about the destruction of their herds."

"And?" Chato prompted.

"And the governor has shown where his true concern lies," she said, her words heavy with irony.

He looked a question.

"The former cattleman, has finally decided to act. He's going to call out the National Guard. After all, no one wants more cattle to be killed."

Their eyes locked ironically.

Chapter 15

"Nothing on the scopes," the private reported.

Colonel Buck Thompson looked at Kate and Chato, who stood nearby, waiting quietly. "You still want to go out?"

"Yes," Kate replied. "I think it's the only way." Chato nodded in silent agreement.

"All right." The colonel turned, nodded to the private, and Kate and Chato followed the two men outside into the night air. Kate breathed deeply, smelling the fragrant desert flowers. Overhead the stars gleamed coldly in the black sky, and around her she sensed the immenseness of the desert. How was she to find these Gila monsters out there?

She shivered in the cool night air and gripped her shoulder bag tightly as Thompson waved to someone driving a jeep. For a moment Chato's hand brushed hers, and she smiled at him.

They climbed into the jeep and the engine roared to life. As the group bounced along, the soldier peered through the starlight scope. He was also monitoring the radio.

"Still nothing, sir. And no reports from up ahead."

"I've deployed the tanks into a semicircle," the colonel explained to Chato and Kate. "The National Guard was mobilized as soon as the governor called me. My boys will be out there." In the moonlight Kate saw that his forehead was beaded with sweat.

We're all afraid, she thought with a slight shiver. She reached out in the darkness for Chato's hand and took some comfort in the enveloping warmth. *We could find them tonight. The giant Gilas. Or they could find us.*

The thought was not reassuring.

It would be the first time they'd seen the large creatures. For a moment a thrill of fear swept through her; then the scientist took over, and she realized that no one else on earth would have a chance to study these animals as she would.

No one else.

As if sensing what she was thinking, Chato touched her cheek with his fingers and she moved her head so that she could kiss them.

"Dammit!"

Startled, they looked toward the front of the jeep. "'Scuse me, ma'am," the colonel said, "but it's those damned journalists."

"What about them?" Kate asked.

"They've hired a bus and are out following my men. And to top it off that fool of a governor's with them!"

Terrance Sylvestor of the *Courier* leaned back in the bus as it jounced along the dirt road in the desert darkness. *The mighty hunters,* he thought wryly remembering how quick the other journalists had beer to suggest the idea.

"A press bus!" they'd exclaimed, and that's what the sign on the flanks of the bus read. And then the governor had somehow managed to turn up before they left Torres. *Very convenient,* Sylvestor told himself.

Signs. Big deal, he thought, shifting positions to be more comfortable. He scratched his knee. Gilas couldn't read, so they wouldn't care if they ate journalists or natives.

He brushed a hand through his brown hair and remembered that day, so short a time ago, when he'd seen Dr. Kate Dwyer with the governor. He should have known something was up; in fact, he had, but he certainly could never have suspected the extent of the story.

He'd been pleased to see her again in Torres, but she hadn't the time of day for him. She was thicker than thieves with that Indian, Chato Del-something or other. In the darkness Sylvestor licked his lips as he recalled the thrust of her breasts against her blouse, the curve of her hips and bottom. Unconsciously, his hand crept to the growing bulge in his pants.

That damned Indian was getting some—

His envious brooding was interrupted by loud laughter from the front of the bus. He frowned as he recognized the braying voice. *The Good Ol' Boy was certainly making points tonight*, he thought. The governor's face would be prominently displayed in newspapers and on TV news by the following day, which certainly wouldn't hurt Roy's campaign effort. *Nothing like free publicity*, Sylvestor thought.

"I talked to Walter this evening, and he can save me a sixty-second spot—"

"I really scooped Dan on this."

"David and John wanted to come, but I was the logical choice."

The voices were filled with pride, certainly boastful. Sylvestor snickered to himself.

He knew why these journalists had been sent on this "big" story. No one else at the networks, the prominent magazines, or the newspapers had wanted to touch it; no one had wanted to come to a backwater state like New Mexico, so the big bosses had sent the second best.

That's what all these men and women were, Sylvestor thought. *Second best*. Even he was, and he knew at well. Second best, or he'd be in some other spot, some place more exciting, like New York, or Washington, or L.A. But he was stuck in this damned state, with its damned friendly natives, and he was wasting the best years of his life.

Wallowing in self-pity, he shut out the noise around him and settled in to nurse his old grudges.

The M60A1 tank from the New Mexico National Guard ground to a halt.

"Where the hell are we?"

"New Mexico," came the laconic reply.

"You asshole, I know *that*."

"Well, you asked."

"Jenkins."

"Yessir?"

"Shut up."

"Yessir."

The tank's commander, Wallace "Walleye" Pennington, a slightly balding insurance salesman in the real world, opened the hatch of the cupola. He rode inside; he didn't like hanging outside, just his head and shoulders sticking out. The motion blew what hair he had left all into snarls, and besides, he'd once lost a hat that way. The wind was always blowing in New Mexico, it seemed, and with it came that blasted stinging sand.

He scratched his stomach and the loose flesh wobbled. He looked around, then used his binoculars to peer into the darkness. He adjusted them, then squinted. Finally he scratched his head, making sure afterward to smooth down the wisps of hair.

'What do you see, sir?"

"Shhh."

Jenkins quieted down. *There was nothing here*, he thought; no one could hear him. Why had Pennington hushed him? He shivered, scowling up at the moon. Why did Levy have to be sick this time? Why couldn't they have got another third man for the tank? Damned inconvenient with only two.

"Goddammit," Pennington said.

"Sir?"

"Get going. Get going quietly."

"Sir?"

"No questions, Jenkins. Get this crate moving."

The tank roared to life and slowly crept forward, smashing the sagebrush, the delicate cactus flowers, the fragile burrows of small animals.

Pennington sat down and rubbed a hand over his face. It was no use. They were lost.

Christ. What was he doing in this outfit? The New Mexico National Guard had a terrible reputation. It got lost; its vehicles collided; it went around and around in circles ... in short, everything they'd done tonight. *Well*, he thought dourly, *at least they hadn't collided with anything ... yet.*

It was, of course, Bev's fault. He shouldn't have listened to her. She'd been the one pushing him into the Reserve. Said she thought he'd look terrific in a uniform. Instead he simply looked balding and fat and middle-aged.

Hell, she was probably shacking up with some guy while he played weekend soldier. And look at him. Skulking about the landscape, looking for, of all things, giant Gila monsters!

Hell, he hadn't seen any of the buggers. If they were so damned big, where the fuck were they?

"Call the others," he instructed Jenkins.

"Yessir." After a moment, "I can't get them, sir."

"Can't?"

"No, sir."

Pennington released an exasperated sigh. "Give me the radio." He fiddled with it—nothing but static. "I know they've got to be out there. I know it."

"Sir?" Very tentatively.

"What?"

"Maybe the Gila monsters got them."

He couldn't see the kid's face in the dark, but he had a good idea it was strained. Like his own. He felt the sweat pop out on his forehead and along his receding hairline.

"Don't be ridiculous, Jenkins. There are no giant Gila monsters. This is simply some ploy by the governor, some military exercise."

"But, sir, on the news tonight—"

"Those damned reporters are communists. You can't believe a word of what they say."

"But Walter Cronkite wouldn't lie!"

"Bullshit!" Pennington turned his attention to the radio once more. "Hello? Anyone out there? Do you read me?"

Nothing.

"I can't stay in here any longer," he said, looking at the confines of the tank. It was closing in on him; he was being stifled. He gasped, choking for air. He ran a hand along his damp collar.

"Sir, do you think you should go outside?" Jenkins said.

"Kid, don't tell me what to do."

"Sir—"

"Shut up, mister."

Pennington stretched and, opening the hatch once more, clambered outside the tank. He looked around as he mopped his face with a crumpled handkerchief. He inhaled deeply. It felt great to be out in the fresh air, away from that dumb tank jock who hadn't changed his socks in a week. Away from—

What was that? He whirled and screamed as the giant shape came smashing, clawing, gnashing down on top of him.

Jenkins heard the terrible shrieks and an awful grinding noise as he cowered, shivering, in the tank. When it was all over, when the tank was no longer being shaken as if by some demonic force, he uncurled his lanky form and cautiously peered outside. When he saw what was left of his commander, he fainted dead away.

———

The dull roar of the tanks split the stillness of the night. There was a sharp crack, then an engine sputtered, died, caught again, and failed once more.

A hatch was thrown back. "Gawddammit!" a voice shouted.

"Where the hell do you think you're going?" another voice demanded.

Two men glared at each other from their respective cupolas.

"You two-assed—"

"Now listen here, you bast—"

Another tank rolled over the crest of the hill. It was followed by another and another and still another. Too late the newcomers tried to brake, for the tanks, one after another, collided until there was a jumble of six of them, all at haphazard angles.

More hatches clanged open as the tank commanders crawled out.

"You mothers," screamed one man, throwing down his cap and glaring at a fellow commander. "Where was your head, up your—"

"Look here, Bennett, I'm not going to take this kind of crap off you."

"Parker, get out here on the double."

"Yessir."

A radioman scrabbled out to join his two tank mates.

Soon the night was filled with the shouting and noisy denunciation of eighteen National Guardsmen. They didn't hear a new sound added to the desert air.

Hissing.

Closer and closer it came, approaching the tanks. Too late one of the men looked up, then pointed.

"Christ!"

The men panicked; some fell; some were trampled. Others tried to clamber back into their tanks, but the large heads, jaws open and dripping greenish ooze, reached down and grabbed the screaming humans. Teeth ground from side to side and bones crunched under the power of the reptilian gnawing. Systematically the Gilas picked off each of the Guardsmen, and in a matter of minutes there was nothing left but bloodstained dirt and a few tatters of cloth that had not been to the monsters' liking.

Having finished their meal, the Gilas turned slowly and left, in search of other game.

"Okay," Colonel Thompson said, "I've sent the flamethrowers on ahead. That should be sufficient for the time being. But first we've got to find that damned press bus. We can't have them wandering around the desert; they'll just get in the way. Damned journalists."

"Makes me glad I didn't major in journalism in college," Chato whispered in Kate's ear. She squeezed his hand in response.

"Communications out, sir," the radio operator called. "With the flamethrowers and now the tanks, sir."

"Damn," said the colonel.

The jeep roared through the night stillness and sped up a steep incline. At the crest, the jeep stopped. Kate and Chato sat up so that they could see beyond the shoulders of the Guardsmen.

Down below on the desert floor, in the moonlight, they could see the National Guard tanks. Six of them. Motionless, they were like statues, and an eerie feeling crept across Kate.

"We'll go on," Thompson said, but his voice was subdued.

She couldn't see Chato's face, but knew it was as strained as her own.

Thompson slowly directed the jeep down until it was parallel with the first tank. Chato and the Guardsman got out and checked the tank. It was empty. They went on to the next. All of the tanks were empty.

"They wouldn't leave," the radio operator said. "Unless they were running for their lives. But surely ..." the colonel's voice trailed off.

"It was the Gilas," Kate said firmly.

Chato stooped and ran his fingers across the dirt. "She's right."

"What?" Thompson asked.

Chato stepped across to the colonel and held out his hand. There were dark streaks on his fingers. Chato sniffed quickly, then said, "Blood. And there's lot of it. Enough for the crews of six tanks."

"My God," Thompson said, his face suddenly ashen.

"Their lair must be found—tonight," Kate said. "The creatures are active right now, but tomorrow, when they're in their burrows, we can come back. And we can get rid of them." She paused. "Before it's, too late."

And her worried eyes met Chato's and Thompson's.

He heard a hissing, like that of a snake, and the bus lurched to one side.

"Flat tire." The whisper swept along the rows of journalists, who stared out the grimy windows, their faces pressed to the cool panes.

"Wall, now, boys—and girls," Governor Roy hastily amended after receiving some hostile looks, "let's help our poor driver by gittin' off this here bus. Let's all see what we kin do."

Once off the bus, Sylvestor lit a cigarette and watched the other journalists.

"—out in the middle of *nowhere*, for Christ's sake!"

"Damned backwater," someone else muttered.

"You wouldn't find this in New York," one of the women-magazine journalists grumbled.

"Nor in Washington," said a well-known commentator who'd had a fall from grace after a long bout with the bottle.

118

No, thought Sylvestor sarcastically, *in those two towns you'd just get mugged.*

"God, it's cold out here. I thought this was the desert! Isn't it supposed to be hot?"

"I can hardly wait to get back to civilization—"

"I hope this makes a damned good story, or my ed is going to have my head."

There were a few chuckles over that. Yet under all the complaints and cynical comments and worldly boredom, there was something else. Fear. They were a long, long way from civilization, and the loneliness and the emptiness of the desert night, and the stark sky above, disconcerted them. But they wouldn't admit the uneasiness; they would simply pretend it didn't exist, and they would go on, talking as though they were attending a cocktail party in Manhattan or Georgetown. Except that they were standing in the middle of the Western wildlands.

No doubt, Sylvestor thought, his lips twisting into a sneer, they thought there'd be the cavalry coming over the hill to save them. *Save them.*

And he shivered.

It was the cold, he told himself quickly. *Only the cold.*

All the lights were on in the bus, and the reporters were now clustered around it like moths.

The wind had risen and brought with it the distinct odor of the desert. Unfamiliar scents that bore no trace of car exhaust or industrial pollution. *Alien*, he thought, *to these Easterners.*

Sand swirled at the journalists' feet, stung their unprotected eyes.

Hiss. Hiss.

Sylvestor, puffing at his second cigarette, cocked his head at the faint noise. Sounded like the tire, the flat tire. But that couldn't be. His eyes flicked to the bus driver and the governor, who were busily engaged in arguing over the tire-changing.

What was it? Sylvestor squinted in the darkness. *Hiss.* A movement. And then yellow lights that blinked. And across the fragrant smell of the desert wafted a strong odor, a stench foul with the rottenness of death.

Hiss.

Over the hill crawled a nightmare. Something large and black against the sky and hill, and behind it appeared more hellish visions.

"Look!" Sylvestor called, pointing. The words were whipped out of his mouth by the wind, and he screamed it again. This time the journalists looked, and there were shrieks from men and women alike.

"Gilas," someone shouted, and the reporters scattered, fleeing in different directions, out into the desert, away from the hell-born monsters.

For creatures so monstrously large, the reptiles moved quickly. Across the sands they crawled.

Sylvestor watched, unable to move, as a giant beaded head struck out, grabbing a woman reporter in its jaws. She cried out in agony as the sharp teeth snapped her spine in two, and her blood and the monster's greenish venom spurted outward in an obscene arc.

Beyond, a Gila had stepped on two wire-service reporters, and beneath the weight of the giant reptile they were crushed into the hard-packed earth, the only sound the pulverization of their bones.

The scenes around Sylvestor were hellish. The nauseating smell of the ooze, dripping from the teeth-encrusted jaws of the Gilas, and the ripe odor of fresh blood, *human* blood, tore at his stomach, clawed at his throat. Bile raced toward his mouth and spewed out onto his shoes and the ground.

Screams filled the air; and all around him he heard the nightmarish sounds of the Gilas as they chewed, and gnawed, and ground, and swallowed, and *devoured.*

As if suddenly released from his inertia, Terrence Sylvestor bolted. He ran, ran away from the nightmare as fast as he could.

Somewhere he heard an agonized, drawn-out cry that sent cold probing fingers down his back, into his groin, and he turned his head back and saw a bullnecked figure being trampled by one of the monsters. And then the creature was chewing on the man, and Sylvestor heard the country tones crying for help.

He ran on.

"Over there," Kate exclaimed. "Do you hear it?"

"Sure do, miss," Thompson said. "Get your gun ready, Ramirez."

The Guardsman nodded silently.

The jeep roared in the night air up another hill and over, and the sand churned beneath the tires. Then it was screaming along, and there was a thud, a cry as the jeep's headlights caught the figure of the man just before the dull *thunk* of a collision.

The jeep skidded and then flipped.

Everything went black momentarily. When Kate opened her eyes, she lay over ten feet from the jeep. It now lay on its side. Within arm's length was Chato, who struggled to a sitting position. He was shaking his head, as if afraid it wasn't there.

"You okay?" she asked. She got slowly and carefully to her feet and moved to him, then sat down unexpectedly as a wave of dizziness bit her.

"Yeah." He crawled to her and ran gentle hands along her arms, body, and legs.

"Nothing's broken," she said. "Just bruised."

"What did we hit?" he asked. "A man, I thought ..."

They got unsteadily to their feet and found the others. The colonel had been thrown onto a large rock. His neck was broken. There was no movement from the National Guard soldier.

Kate put a hand to her face and said nothing.

"Great," Chato said. "We're in the middle of the desert at night. Miles from everywhere."

"Listen." Kate grabbed his arm and shook it.

Hiss. Hiss.

Chato ran for Ramirez's gun.

Hiss.

The sound came closer. The Gila monster. Kate stared at it, mesmerized.

She had never seen anything like it. In the moonlight it was almost all black, the orange almost invisible. She could smell the rank odor of its venom. She'd never seen any living creature as large as this, as *intent*, as evil. And it knew she was there; it was coming after her.

Yet she couldn't run from this. It was wonderful. It was beautiful. So large, yet compact for its size. The gleaming beadlike skin. *It was almost jeweled*, she thought. *It was a monarch—the king of land creatures.*

She walked toward it, aware of nothing except this giant reptile.

"Run," Chato screamed as the creature crawled toward her.

A shot sounded from behind her, but the Gila monster kept advancing. And then suddenly she was free of her hypnosis. She turned and ran.

"C'mon," Chato called. She stumbled past a body, gave it a quick glance, and saw a pale face and hollowed eyes. There was something familiar about it, but her mind couldn't identify it, not at that moment.

She ran on. Chato grabbed her hand, and now they were both running away.

"There!" He pointed. A squat shape loomed some yards from them, a blackness in the moonlight. Fenced with warning Signs. STAY OUT. HIGH VOLTAGE. DANGER.

Chato turned and shot once more at the reptile. It hissed at him, and its long sinuous tongue flicked out. Again he shot at the creature. There was a thud as the bullet struck the beaded skin, but the animal only seemed enraged. It hissed louder, and venom splashed onto the ground. It drew closer.

Beyond it there was a second giant reptile.

Chato pushed Kate down in a mound of sand, then ran toward the power station. He fired another shot from the rifle and the creature turned toward him. Slowly it came forward, its head searching from side to side, looking for the irritant.

The second lizard followed some yards behind. Chato fired at the first lizard again and it began crawling his way. He stepped behind the wire fence of the power station and shot again, carefully, deliberately, at the creature.

Hissing filled the air as the reptile pushed against the fence. The wire strained, then buckled like cardboard, and the creature advanced. It hit the electrical wiring, and there was a blue crackle, then sparks flew.

Boom! The station exploded, flames leaping into the sky. White lightning crept along the lizard's body and here was a sizzling sound. It hissed, then squealed. Its yellow eyes blinked as though it were suffering great pain, and it gave a great moan. The reptile's head jerked upward, the blunt snout pointing heavenward.

Then with a thump it fell inside the fence, and lay still.

Chato ran back toward Kate and dived into the sand beside her. They kept very still, while the second Gila monster circled the burning power station. It hissed. It drooled its nauseating venom. It bent its head, peering at the charred carcass of its companion. Slowly it turned and lumbered away. Then it was past the station and out into the desert, away from the couple.

When he could no longer see the creature in the moonlight, Chato grabbed Kate's hand.

"Let's just wait here," he said. "I'd like to run like hell, but—"

"But," she whispered, "we don't know what's out there." She shivered, and he put an arm around her.

"No," he said, drawing closer to her. The long wait for the end of night began.

Chapter 16

Early in the morning, once back in Torres, they reported to the police and National Guard Headquarters what had happened the night before, then were taken to a first-aid station.

Kate had bruises and a cracked rib, while Chato had sustained no more than some scrapes along his arms and legs.

"Us tough Indians," he said, then yelped as the doctor applied iodine to his scrapes.

"Yes, real tough," Kate said with a faint smile.

It was midmorning before they returned to the motel room. Without removing their sandy clothes, they fell into bed, wrapped in each other's arms.

It was late afternoon when Kate awoke. She stretched, then grimaced, feeling the soreness shoot through her arms and legs. Her head throbbed, her ribs ached, and the inside of her mouth felt like sandpaper. She glanced over at Chato.

He lay with one arm flung over his face, and she could see the puffiness on his cheeks and chin from having been thrown onto the ground. Sand dotted his black hair, and she reached over and brushed some away.

"Ummh," he said, then moaned.

"Good morning." She yawned as his eyes opened. "Only I suppose it's afternoon."

"Ooof."

"Communicative, aren't we?"

"No. Sore."

Slowly sitting up, he swung his legs over the side of the double bed, then sat there with his head in his hands. "Why do I feel like I've been *fighting* the entire U.S. cavalry?"

"I think that would have been easier," Kate said lightly. "Let's shower."

"Together?" He grinned.

"Together. We may not be able to do anything more than hold each other up."

"That's okay with me."

"C'mon," she said, and began pulling off her dirty clothes, each article left behind in a trail to the bathroom.

An hour later, clean and freshly dressed, they went across the street to the small coffee shop. As they sat down to a breakfast of hash browns, bacon, eggs, toast, and coffee, Kate said, "We can't kill them with guns."

"I noticed," Chato said. He took a sip of coffee. "What do you suggest?"

"I don't know. I've got to think about this. I was so sure that we would get them last night, that they could be destroyed by bullets." She rubbed her face wearily. "I think maybe we should visit the governor in the next day or so."

Chato nodded. His eyes narrowed as he read something a few feet away from the counter. "Better make your appointment with the lieutenant governor," he suggested.

"Why?"

He nodded to the screaming black headlines on the evening newspaper across from him.

"GOVERNOR DIES IN GILA ATTACK," it read.

Wordlessly, Kate stared at Chato.

What was she to do? Kate asked herself. It was *her* responsibility. She had to find a way to destroy the creatures. Yet … yet, she would like to study one them. Alive.

There hadn't been much left of the Gila that had attacked the power station. What little she could salvage from the charred mess had been sent, refrigerated, to her lab at the university. She would take a look at it later, when she had the proper facilities. Down here it was too primitive, the threat from the others too immediate.

She paced the motel room, pausing now and then to look out the window. For the first time in days there were no reporters outside. *Of course*, she told herself, *there were no reporters left alive, either*.

How to stop the Gilas? Bullets didn't appear to work; fire had stopped one, but on a large scale, wasn't fire impractical? Fire could get out of hand. So could poison. What was left? She didn't know.

As he walked around the town, Chato observed the signs of nervousness so evident the day after the governor's death.

It wasn't, Chato reasoned, that anyone grieved particularly for Bubba J. Roy; the sad thing was that no one really did. The townsfolk of Torres were simply in a state of shock after last night's slaughter.

And slaughter was the only word for it. The governor and five of his top aides had been killed. The bus driver, some hapless employee of a charter firm, had died. Also dead were newspaper reporters, television personalities, cameramen and -women, and journalists from television, newspapers, and magazines. Dead. Some forty-three of them. And all the Guardsmen as well.

The only survivor, in fact, besides Kate and Chato, had been an Albuquerque reporter, Terrance Sylvestor, now hospitalized. He had been the man whom their jeep had struck.

The horrible irony, Chato thought as he walked along Torres' main street, his hands thrust into the pockets of his jeans, was that this man had survived the deadly attack of the giant Gila monsters, only to be knocked down in the wide-open desert by a National Guard jeep. Sylvestor had been in critical condition when he was flown to the hospital only hours before.

Three survivors—that was all. Chato looked around and thought how empty the town seemed today. No trace of the previous day's carnival atmosphere. The vendors' stands were deserted, their pennants drooping forlornly.

Church services had been going on all day, even though it wasn't Sunday. Services for the dead, for the living, for deliverance.

He turned and headed back to the motel.

"I think I've got the key to defeating these reptiles," Kate said.

Joaquin Barela, the Acting Governor, lifted a supercilious eyebrow. "Oh, do you, ... Doctor?" The tone of his voice indicated he didn't care much what Dr. Dwyer thought. He was old-stock Spanish, lean and bearded like a pirate. In his background the opinions of women didn't count for much.

She leaned forward intently. "These animals are mutants, as you no doubt realize," she said. "But they're still essentially reptiles. As such they're cold-blooded. It takes the heat of the sun to warm their bodies enough for them to even move. I theorize that's why they attack by night; they have to lie up during the day, restoring their body heat."

Barela riffled through a stack of casualty reports from the Otero County disaster. Ignoring his rudeness, Kate continued. "The Gilas are almost certainly vulnerable to cold." She paused. "I think we should freeze them."

"*Freeze* them?"

"Yes. Drop canisters of some liquid gas—liquid oxygen. Or better yet nitrogen. Even if the cold isn't intense enough to freeze them completely, it would certainly immobilize them. And then the

Army can destroy them with explosives or whatever." *We might even capture a few alive, for study*, the scientist in her said.

A look of astonishment crossed Barela's face. He looked hard at Kate, over at Chato and back at the woman. "You're joking."

"The lady wouldn't joke about this," Chato said.

"It's the only method I can think of that won't cause irreparable ecological damage," Kate said.

Barela rubbed his hands precisely against one another, then paused momentarily as he appeared to carefully select his words. "I've heard enough of this nonsense," he said. "Freezing the Gilas. My God, woman, are you seriously suggesting we turn the state of New Mexico into a giant cold-storage locker?" Kate started to interrupt. He cut her off with a sharp gesture of his hand. "Although I don't know why I'm wasting the time, Dr. Dwyer, I will tell you exactly what I am doing to do. I am going to call the Air Force and ask for saturation bombing of the Gilas." He thought for a moment. "Napalm should do nicely, I believe."

"But you can't!" Kate shouted. "My God, don't you know what that would do to the countryside? The ecological balance of the desert is fragile, incredibly so. Fire would burn off the ground cover for miles around. There would be nothing to check erosion, the animal population would die off for lack of food and shelter—"

"It's the *human* population we're concerned with, Dr. Dwyer." He smiled thinly. "Perhaps you should don a black armband and join the environmentalists protesting our persecution of the Gilas."

"But extreme cold—"

"I put my faith in napalm, Doctor."

"So did our generals in Vietnam," Chato said. His voice had an edge Kate had never heard before, and he Apache's eyes were bleak. "Worked real well for them, didn't it?"

Barela turned red. A slim finger stabbed a button on his telephone console. "Miss Garcia," he said to the secretary's tinny reply, "kindly escort Dr. Dwyer and Dr. Del-Klinne from my office, if you will."

"What are you going to do?" Chato asked Kate as the door of the politician's office opened and a petite Chicana stared up at them.

"Nothing," Kate said bitterly. "You can't fight city hall, no matter how stupid it is."

She turned on her heel and marched past the secretary, who quickly jumped out of the way to avoid being touched by Chato.

Chapter 17

The night was so black, Chato thought. He glanced out the window of the Huey helicopter, then at Kate, who sat staring ahead at the pilot, their escort that night.

He glanced down at the white sea of sand in the moonlight. *Down there,* he thought, down there they might find those creatures.

Then he glanced back at Kate. She was so sure the lizards' lair was down there.

A shadow flitted by. A Phantom fighter, up from Holloman Air Force Base, he knew, watching the orange glow from the twin exhausts. A Phantom to survey the area, find the monsters, and then bomb them into oblivion. All on the orders of the lieutenant governor.

Yet already, since he and Kate had visited Barreras, protests had been raised from the environmentalists, the Tourism Board of New Mexico, the Sierra Club, the National Forest Service, and the ranchers, who claimed that valuable grazing land would be destroyed if the air force bombed White Sands and the surrounding areas. Ordinary bombs were bad enough, Chato reflected, but the Phantom fighters carried napalm.

Jellied gasoline, it would ignite on contact and burn across an already bone-dry landscape. Prairie fires. Fires that would sweep across miles and miles of the land. Miles and miles.

For an instant his mind leaped back through the years, and he could see the flames, hear the cries, smell the singed flesh and burning vegetation. 'Nam. In the distance was the whine of aircraft. Over that could be heard the cries and screams of those dying. He felt his body tense, heard the cock of the rifle, waited, not breathing, waiting ...

The helicopter dipped a little and Kate grabbed Chato's arm. The pressure of her fingers brought his mind back to the present, and for a moment, confused, he blinked in the darkness of the helicopter, wondering where he was.

But when he glanced out the window, he knew again. New Mexico. Looking for the giant Gila monsters. He smiled suddenly. Who would have thought he'd be facing something like this? It was so absurd; it was so serious.

"Look," Kate said, and pointed.

"That's them, ma'am," the pilot, Captain Jake Grant, confirmed.

Chato looked out the window and whistled silently.

Across the sands came the huge lizards. They fanned across the earth, black shadows crawling along on powder white. Their black-and-orange hides shone in the night, and even from the height of the helicopter Chato could see the yellow of their eyes, like the flickering of evil fires. His imagination thus loosened, he felt he could almost hear their combined hissing over the whirling of the Huey's blades.

Across the desert floor the monsters advanced, and Chato pitied anything—anyone—in their path.

"There they go," Grant said unnecessarily.

Dark shapes fell across the sky, swooping downward like huge birds of prey. The irony, Chato thought, was that the Phantoms had what was called standard lizard camouflage. Lizard camouflage for the destruction of the lizards. *Why not?* he asked himself. It made as much sense as any of this.

Then there was the impact of the napalm bombs and the bursting of the flame. On the desert below, the vegetation caught fire, burning in the night. A hundred small bonfires blazed, then crept slowly across the dry desert, igniting the paper-dry plants.

More napalm bombs fell. Across the radio came the cool and crackly voices of the various Phantoms. Chato tried to listen, but couldn't make out any individual comments.

"They can't live through that," Captain Grant said smugly. He smiled at the two, then winked at Kate, whose lips curved into a faint smile. "There'll be another load dropped—just in case some survived. Better to do the mopping up now than later."

Chato watched as more napalm rained. More death, more destruction. But no, he told himself, they had to do this, to prevent the Gilas from marching northward.

Some fires burned and then flickered out. Others continued to spread, fanned by a slight nighttime breeze. Flames leaped up as the fire touched more plants.

Between the fires, something moved.

"Gilas," Kate said, her voice emotionless.

"It can't be," the pilot whispered.

"It is."

"But how?" the Air Force man asked, and Chato knew that he needed to know, needed to win over the animals. Man had to be shown superior. Right. *Wrong*, Chato thought dourly, watching the Gilas continue their advance.

"Gilas can burrow into the ground in a matter of seconds," Kate said. "They must have survived that way."

"The bombing was so quick," Grant said. "Some of them should have died. Some." There was a note of desperation in his voice, a desperation reflected on all their faces.

Kate shrugged. "Maybe a few slower ones. Perhaps some of the older ones, or the young Gilas. But the main force, I'm afraid, is still there."

Grant reached across and spoke into the radio. There was a crackle in response; then a voice, low yet with horror underlying it, spoke to him.

"I've explained," Grant said. "They're going to drop more napalm."

"It's not going to work," Chato said. "It didn't just now."

"They're going to try," the pilot said simply.

They listened to the whine of the Phantoms, then Kate gasped and pointed again. "Headlights. On the desert."

"What the hell?" Captain Grant spoke quickly into the radio again. He listened for a moment, then replied.

Chato, glancing out a window, watched one of the fighter-bombers break away from the group and swoop toward the ground. In a few minutes the plane rejoined the others.

The radio crackled to life once more. Grant looked at them and shook his head. "It's those damned environmentalists in their bus, banner and all."

"Don't they realize they could get killed?" Kate asked.

Grant shrugged. "I guess they think we won't bomb if they're down there."

"Will you?"

"Hell, no. It's hard enough being in the military these days, without being sued for murder."

The headlights below flickered, and then the shadows crept closer.

"Those fools," Captain Grant said bitterly.

"You can't even bomb the lizards to protect the environmentalists," Chato said.

"Hell, we ought to bomb those do-gooders anyway. Take care of the pack of 'em." He was silent for a moment, then: "I've radioed ahead. Help is on the way. I think they'll be too late, though. Damned lot of fools."

Below the circling helicopter, Chato could see the black carpet of lizards, and beyond them the small shape of the bus. Even smaller objects came out. He could imagine them waving placards. Probably "SAVE OUR GILAs," "PROTECT NATURE FROM MAN."

They were meddlers. And very soon they were going to be dead meddlers, unless they had sense enough to get back in their bus and hightail it out of there. But he doubted they would.

More conversation came over the radio, and the pilot listened, then spoke a few words into it. He slammed his hand down.

"They bought it. The Gilas got them. So much for their signs and protests. Now we're going to bomb those lizards out of existence."

Kate, who had remained silent, turned to look at Chato. She started to speak but he shook his head.

Down the napalm bombs rained, hundreds of bombs dropping onto the sand. The desert floor became a torrent of fire, reaching far up into the night sky. Everywhere there was red and orange and yellow, flames that threatened to consume everything, even the world, Chato thought. *Hell must look something like this*, he told himself as he watched sparks shoot from fiery fingers of flame. He thought of the small animals running from the fire, or those that were trapped. He thought of the rare vegetation, the cacti, the nightflowers that bloomed there but were now seared. *It had to be done*, he told himself. It had to be. The Gilas had to be stopped.

The fires spread across the desert, a band of crimson and sulfur that seemed to encompass the universe. For what seemed like hours the napalm bombs fell and fell, drenching the desert with the gasoline. Finally the hellish rain ended. Only the flickering raging fires remained.

Their pilot cheered, and yet there was almost a current of fear underneath. "We got those bastards for sure this time!"

135

"Let's go back," Kate said, weariness in her voice. She pushed back a strand of her hair and touched Chato's hand.

She's disappointed, he thought. She wanted a sample, more than the charred lizard ... she wanted one of those giant reptiles, and now they're gone. *The pure scientist*, he thought, but not really understanding.

The lizards were a menace, the enemy, and they had to be killed—each and every one.

"Jesus," Grant whispered.

"What is it?" Fatigue made her voice sharp.

"Jesus," Grant repeated, and he pointed with one trembling finger.

Chato and Kate followed his direction.

The Gilas were not dead; they were very much alive and continuing their northward march.

Chapter 18

*H*iss. Hiss. Hiss.

Separated from its companions, it burrowed through the sand and the dirt. Farther down it went, deeper and deeper.

Hiss!

It was an emphatic sound, as in a shower of sand and dirt the creature dropped onto a hard surface. The suddenness of bright track lights all around it blazed in its eyes, blinding it momentarily, and it blinked rapidly.

Hiss.

Wary, the creature twisted its head from side to side, its long tongue flicking out. The tongue touched the coldness of steel, the roughness of cement.

It crawled forward, along the parallel railings of steel. It left a trail of greenish ooze. Ahead of the creature there was a shout. Men in uniforms ran forward. Someone shouted a command.

Hiss. Hiss.

The soldiers lifted their M-16 rifles and fired at the giant lizard. Ricocheting off the beaded hide, the bullets tumbled, squealing hellish counterpoint to the hissing of the Gila monster.

Down the track, a long way from the immense creature, gleamed a metallic object. As long as the lizard; unmoving; silent.

Hiss.

The jaws of the Gila ground sideways, splashing out more of the sticky venom.

It advanced on that cold object, oblivious to the humans around it who were still shooting.

It hissed louder as one of the bullets finally embedded itself in a worn patch of beady hide. It growled deep in its throat, but kept moving.

On and on it came, toward the men, toward the Polaris ICBM, toward the nuclear warhead.

The bullets rained on its hide, as the napalm bombs had rained on the surface, the fiery surface the creature had fled. Around it squealed more of the bullets.

It was lost; it sought its own kind; it crawled on and on.

Slowly the thing slowed as the bullets found their way into its hide. One flew into its right eye, and the eye exploded, clear liquid seeping down the creature's blunt snout. It screamed, a shrill sound in the silo, silencing the men and their machines.

Another round of bullets flew, seeking its vulnerable head. The tongue flicked out, was cut in half by a torrent of metal. It screamed again.

Unable to move any longer, paralyzed, bleeding in more than a dozen places, its right eye a bloody socket, the Gila halted, then collapsed on the warhead of the Polaris missile.

It died even as the soldiers came running down the trackway, ready to pump out the propellant and oxidizer, lest the fuel blow up the silo and the surrounding countryside.

Chapter 19

"Oh, my God," the airman said. He pointed, and the lieutenant whirled.

Across the cement runways of Holloman Air Force base, from out of the desert night, crawled an army of giant Gila monsters.

A fighter jet, at the point of taking off, hurtled down the runway. Suddenly one of the creatures crept forward and raised its massive head. The F-111 brushed against it, wobbled, spun, and then bit the earth, bursting a ban of flames.

"Get going!" the lieutenant shouted to the airman. Without waiting to see what the other man did, the young officer ran back to the headquarters. Holloman had to be warned, had to be evacuated before these creatures destroyed everything.

"Jesus," Jesus," he kept muttering to himself, and it was almost a litany.

From behind him he could hear the explosions of the planes that couldn't swerve, couldn't miss the giant lizards. Above that he heard the hellish hissing of the lizards, and the cries and screams of the men in the planes.

The drogue chute popped as the jet fighter taxied down the runway. The pilot looked up from his control panel and paled at what he saw ahead.

139

The thing loomed up before him, and he tried to take the plane to the right to avoid colliding with it. But it was too late. The creature was too long, too immense, and he was coming in too fast.

There was a thud as metal impacted flesh; sparks like the angry corona of a miniature sun, shot outward. The hissing of the creature filled his head, and he wanted to put his hands over his ears to shut out the noise. He struggled with the canopy, but it jammed shut. The manufacturers of the plane had envisioned many exigencies, but never anything like this!

Above the pilot the head of the giant Gila wobbled from side to side as it stared malevolently in at him. He could see the evil yellow eyes regarding him, thick ooze draining out of the yard-wide mouth. Flame flickered along the hull of his jet as he struggled to get out.

He had to make it; Sharon was expecting him. She would have dinner waiting; she would hug him, ask him how the day had gone. And he would have to see her ... just once more.... He hadn't said that morning that he loved her. Why had he left in such hurry? Why?

There was a boom that filled his head and the cockpit, and he knew that he was too late, that he wouldn't get out in time. At least, he thought, watching the flames shoot up around him, he would have the satisfaction of knowing that he'd taken one of the bastards with him. It might make up for his death. It might.

The creatures toppled walls and fences; swing set and lampposts fell like toothpicks before the advance of the giant lizards. The walls of houses bulged in, the collapsed as the Gilas kept on moving.

Mess halls, recreation centers, administration buildings—nothing withstood the battering of the enraged lizards. Nothing, no one, stood in their path.

Sharon lit the candles, then stepped back to gaze at the crystal- and silver-set table. The candlelight gave the darkened room a cheering, romantic light, and she nodded in approval.

Bob would too, she thought, and smiled. He would be landing anytime now; within the next ten minutes the door would burst open and he would call her name, then stride out to the kitchen to grab her about the waist and kiss her ear. The way he had done each evening for the past five years of their marriage.

She went back out into the kitchen to check on the roast. She happened to glance out the kitchen windows as she closed the oven door, and she frowned at what he saw.

What was that light? Fire? She went to the sink and stared out through the panes into the darkness. It *was* fire. She whirled around to go to the telephone. The fire marshal should be alerted; something had to be done.

There was a crash in the living room, then silence. "Bob?" she called.

Silence again, then a scrabbling.

Feeling a chill prickle down her spine, she walked out of the kitchen into the dining room, and then into the small living room.

"Bob?"

She frowned, turned on a lamp.

She screamed as the wall of her house bulged in, collapsed, and two pairs of evil, intent yellow eyes stared in at her.

The lone man crawled across the runway and stared at the ruins of the air base. Burning planes, looking like dead insects, lay at grotesque angles, smashed where they had stood. Around them were the smoldering carcasses of the giant Gila monsters that had been caught in the conflagrations.

He could hear the cry of those humans trapped, those burned, those dying.

Everywhere he looked he saw flames and heard the awful hissing.

The Gilas weren't gone yet. Tears formed in his smoke-reddened eyes as he watched the destruction continue around him.

The greatest air force in the world, and they couldn't do a damned thing about these monsters. The napalm hadn't killed them, and they had just crawled onto Holloman to avenge the attempt against them.

What was mankind to do? the injured man wondered. How would they win? What was left? Nuclear weapons? Would they use nuclear weapons to rid themselves of these horrible creatures, these all-too real chimeras? Use those bombs and there would be nothing left of New Mexico, of the Southwest—nothing but dead land. But then, he thought bitterly, people living in the hives on both coasts wouldn't care, wouldn't understand; and those hopelessly bureaucratic minds in Washington certainly wouldn't be concerned.

Nuke the Gilas, he thought, passing one hand over his face. *Nuke them. Before ... before they destroy us.*

He watched in disbelief now as the Gilas, those that were left of the original column that had attacked Holloman, turned slowly and vanished into the darkness from which they had come.

He heard the terrified cries of injured and lost children, and watched helplessly as a little girl, her dress all bloody and torn, ran past him, shrieking, as if pursued by some unseen creature. She was, he knew, and would be for the rest of her life. His eyes closed briefly as a shudder ran through him.

Would he be able to forget it, this carnage? Would he be able to forget the sight of the leveled building, the half-eaten corpses strewn about the runways and streets of the base, the pools of sickening venom and the dogs that had lapped at them? Could he forget the screams, the cries, the moaning, the hissing?

No.

The Gilas have done what they'd come to do, he told himself. *They're paying us back for what we did to them … what we tried to do.*

But they've done it better. And we're the ones who are suffering …

He slowly got to his feet and staggered forward, the blood oozing from his burns, and began looking for the little girl.

Chapter 20

Hand in hand, Kate and Chato returned to the Golden Palomino Motel. They entered their room quietly, and Chato moved across the floor and switched on a light.

He sat on the bed, its old springs sagging beneath his weight. "God." He put his head in his hands.

Without a word, Kate closed and locked the door, then walked into the bathroom. She turned on the light and looked in the mirror.

There were dark smudges under her eyes, as though all her mascara had flaked off. But she knew it wasn't that. Her eyes were bloodshot, too, and tears had run down her cheeks, leaving twin furrows in her makeup. Her hair had come down, straggled about her face. She looked haggard, old. *Frightened*, she thought.

Running cold water into the cracked basin, she splashed it on her face and hands and ran a damp washcloth across her throat and neck. She dried her face on the white towel; her makeup left streaks. She didn't care. Crumpling the cloth, she threw it across the bathroom.

When she came out, Chato was lying across the bed, on his back. One arm was flung over his eyes.

The phone began ringing. He started to reach for it.

"Don't." Her voice was harsh. "Don't, Chato. Not now." Sitting down beside him, she touched his face. She wanted to touch him,

144

have him touch her. "I don't want them to know were here yet. Not now. Okay?"

He nodded and stared up at her. His eyes were as bloodshot as hers, she thought, and his face was serious, the grimmest she'd ever seen it.

Bending down, Kate pressed her lips to his. His mouth opened up and his tongue traced the line of her lips. She moaned and put her arms around him. Then she was lying next to him, and he was kissing her on the face, on the neck. She ripped open her blouse, tore off her pants, and watched as he carefully got out of his jeans and shirt and boots.

"Hurry," she said, a note of urgency in her voice.

He nodded.

She saw he was ready for her, and she trembled. She wanted him now. *Now*, dammit.

Then he was on her, his solid body so warm and *there* against hers. She caressed his chest, feeling the smoothness; his arms; stroked his firm buttocks, felt them tightening at the touch of her hand.

His hand explored the soft area between her thighs, and she moaned, opening her legs. She was becoming warmer and moister, and she wanted him *now*, wanted him in her.

Without speaking, Chato thrust deep inside her. She growled, and he smiled, but it was a smile without humor. Their bodies rocked as one, silently, purposefully, and there were no words. The movements became more frenzied, almost frantic. Faster and faster, until at last she gripped his shoulders with fingers that were like talons, and he cried out.

There was just the single cry in the motel room, held in the air for a moment and then gone.

He collapsed on her, nestling his head on her shoulder. She stroked the long silky black hair, touched his high cheekbones.

Then tears welled up in her eyes and streamed down her cheeks. She tried to push them away with one hand, but more came back to replace them.

He reached over and gently kissed her. Her arms tightened around him, and he muttered low in his throat.

She couldn't tell what he said, but it wasn't important. Somehow the unheard words were reassuring. She closed her eyes, and slowly the tears stopped.

A long time afterward they dressed, as silently as they had undressed. Chato picked up the phone.

"Any calls?" He listened, then began jotting something down on the pad by the bed. "Yeah. Okay." There were several minutes of silence, then, "Send him over when you can."

He put the phone receiver back on its cradle and looked at her. She had poured two glasses of wine from a bottle they had bought earlier. She wished now that it was something stronger.

"Here, drink this."

"Thanks."

He drained his glass, then held it out for more. She complied.

"What's up?"

"More reports coming in. The Sheriff's office is sending a messenger over with copies for us."

"When's he coming?"

"In a few minutes, I guess." He put the pillows against the headboard and leaned back against them. He stared down at his bare feet, then held out his empty glass again.

"Don't get drunk," she admonished gently.

His black eyes simply stared at her.

She filled the glass and was preparing to pour more wine for herself when there was a knock at the door. "Who is it?" she called.

"Freddy from the sheriff's office," came a voice.

She unlocked the door and let the tall, lanky boy in. She saw his eyes, riveted on Chato, and she could well imagine his thoughts. A white woman and an Indian. And God knows what they were doing.

Briefly a smile touched Kate's lips. She ran a hand through her hair, suddenly aware again of how awful she looked.

"Well?" she prompted, as the boy continued to stare.

"Here're your reports, m-ma'am," he stuttered slightly, and handed her a manila folder.

"Thank you," Kate said.

"Uh, thank you, ma'am—er—Doctor." He backed quickly out of the room, and she locked the door behind him. She opened the folder, handed some of the papers to Chato, and began going through the reports.

Holloman Air Force Base had been virtually destroyed by the creatures ... only a small group of aircraft had not been damaged — those that had been flying that night. Ranch after ranch in the desert had been demolished ... the death count now stood in the thousands.

Thousands dead from these giant creatures ... and maybe hundreds of thousands, she told herself, if the Gilas reached Albuquerque.

But how could they stop them? Napalm hadn't worked. The Gilas seemed impervious to bullets, and the lieutenant governor — acting governor, she corrected herself automatically—didn't seem particularly amenable to her plan for using liquid nitrogen. Short of nuclear weapons, what was left?

She watched as Chato read through the papers. He frowned, sighing deeply.

The ringing of the telephone startled both of them. Chato picked it up, listened, nodded once, and said, "Goddammit." Then silence again. "I'll tell her." He hung up and looked at Kate.

"What is it?" she demanded.

"I was right," he replied. "They are going northward. Gilas have been spotted on the highway to Albuquerque."

Chapter 21

"All the roads have been closed between here and the city," Chato went on. "And they plan to evacuate the city if the Gilas can't be stopped."

"Damn," she said, standing, and her voice broke. "Damn." The tears were back again, hot and profuse. She brushed at them angrily.

"Hey," he said, suddenly standing by her side, and slipped his arms around her. "What's the matter, Kate?"

She shook her head wordlessly, then leaned against him and cried. Her body shook from the sobbing, and she felt his arms tighten around her. He felt so warm, so strong. Secure.

He let her cry, and finally her sobbing stopped, fading into a pathetic half-crying, half-hiccupping sound. She trembled, then opened her eyes and stared up at him.

His expression was so encouraging. "I—I—" She stopped. How could she say anything to him? How? Especially this—it was so close to her, it was *her*. But secret. So secret.

"Yes?"

"I feel so ineffectual," she said.

"We all do."

"But they have to be stopped."

"You can't do it alone," he pointed out.

"I'm not suggesting that I can." She broke away from him, from the grip that now seemed binding, and sipped some wine, then sat on one corner of the bed. She stared down at the floor, the cracks in the wood—in her life, her world, she thought dully. She looked up. Chato was still standing there, waiting for her to speak.

"I'm not suggesting that," she said again.

"Then what are you suggesting?"

"I have to stop them. It *is* my responsibility. The governor came to me. I came down here. And now I've blown it."

"You've what?"

"I've blown it."

"Listen, Kate"—he swung his face close to hers—"I don't want to hear any of this self-deprecating garbage. It's not like you, and it's a bunch of bullshit. I just won't take it."

"I am not—" she began.

"You are."

"Look." She spoke deliberately. "I do have to do something. I know that this invasion by the Gilas isn't my fault. I know also that it's not my fault they haven't been stopped. But I have to follow through. *I* have to be concerned. I have to—"

"And you don't think I'm concerned?" he demanded.

"No. Yes. I mean—"

"Look, Kate, just because you're an internationally known scientist doesn't mean you have the corner market on all sorts of human reactions. I won't have you carting all this guilt around when you can't do a single blessed thing."

"But I can."

"What's that?"

"I'm going to call the acting governor. He has no choice now. He has to listen to me, or else he's a fool."

"No matter what, I think he's a fool," Chato said. "I just hope he'll be struck with some common sense for once."

150

Kate picked up the phone. "Collect to Santa Fe, please." She smiled at Chato. "At least he can pay for the blasted call."

It was a few minutes before she could convince the operator at the state capitol building to accept the call, but at last she was put through to the proper office.

"Hello, Governor Barela? Kate Dwyer here. Yes, I know." She waited, then took a deep breath and glanced once at Chato, who smiled reassuringly. "Sir, you have to take my earlier suggestion seriously now. There is no other choice; you must realize that. Yes." A pause, then, "Of course. Tomorrow morning. That would be fine. Thank you, six." She hung up and turned to face Chato.

"Well?"

"He conceded."

"Maybe there's hope for him after all."

"He agreed with what I said. In fact, he started out saying that himself, that he had no choice but to follow my plan. And he said he would act at once."

"Lesser of the two evils, I guess."

"Chato!"

"Sorry." He shrugged, a rueful look on his face. "What else did he have to say?"

"We're being flown to Kirtland in Albuquerque tomorrow—we're overseeing the preparations."

"Good." Chato smiled. "Then I suggest we get a good night's rest."

Kate smiled in return. "I don't know about the rest part, but I know it's going to be good."

Chato chuckled and turned out the lights.

Chapter 22

Like prehistoric monsters the bombers squatted in the heat-shimmer of the runway. Blue trucks crawled between the behemoths, tending to their needs, while mechanics scurried back and forth like insects. Despite the heat, Chato shivered. In 'Nam he had seen enough B-52s to last him a lifetime. Still, it was appropriate: set monsters to kill monsters.

"The Sandia Corporation people were very cooperative." General Donald Adlerson, the base commander, sat with Kate and Chato in the incongruous cool of his limousine. "They've made up several hundred special canisters, pressurized and refrigerated to hold the liquid nitrogen."

"But the noise," Kate said. "The Gilas heard the Phantoms and burrowed. Won't the noise disturb them?"

Adlerson gestured grandly at the winged dinosaurs. "These babies'll bomb from twenty thousand feet," he said, smiling, "and those monsters won't know what hit them."

Kate nodded dubiously, watching the frenetic activity as the bombers were readied for their mission. She doubted the base had seen this much activity since the end of the Vietnam War.

And now the threat, she told herself, *was not the North Vietnamese, nor the Russians, nor the Chinese, but a product of nature itself—and man's arrogance.*

Giant Gila monsters. Who would ever have thought that Kirtland would be put on alert because of lizards? It was so ironic, she told herself, that she could almost laugh out loud or, as tears suddenly filled her eyes, cry.

What was wrong with her? The Gilas had to be stopped. Every night they crept closer to Albuquerque and the large human population there. If the Gilas weren't destroyed, then Albuquerque would be in ruins.

But the Gilas, the Gilas, she told herself. There had never been anything like them. Mutations … when ever again would anyone—would she—be able to study something as marvelous as the giant Gilas?

Marvelous, but terrible.

She was aware that General Adlerson was saying something.

"—It's been a lot of work, but I think we've done it quite quickly and efficiently."

Chato murmured something she didn't catch. He wasn't very enthusiastic about being on the base; he hadn't said much since last night. She wondered what his thoughts were. She knew that he didn't care much for the military, but also that it transcended that. She caught his concerned eyes on her, and she gave him what she hoped was a reassuring smile.

"Here we are," the general announced. The military car pulled to a stop, and the general leaped out and held the door for Kate.

She thanked him as she climbed out, then looked around. On the runways she saw the B-52 bombers at rest. *Like giant birds of carrion*, she thought suddenly. Appropriate. Birds to attack the lizards.

In the slight overcast of the day she could see the lights at the wing tips. The fish-white belly of the bombers reminded her of lizards, and that too was ironic.

She pushed a curl of red hair behind her ear and turned to look at the general, who was surveying the planes with pride.

"Damned good job they did," he said.

"I have no doubt of that, General," she responded.

Chato said nothing, merely squinting against the rays of the sun that broke through the clouds at that moment.

"Would you care to see them?" the general asked, smiling at Kate.

He was flirting, and she really didn't feel in the mood. "No, thank you, sir. I'll just have to take your word that they're efficient. I'm no military expert and would hardly know what to look for." But she softened her words with a smile. There was no use in making him angry.

He smiled in response. "What about you, Mr. Del—Chato?"

"No. Thanks."

Chato seemed wrapped up in his own world today, and Kate wondered if he was remembering the war. He didn't say a lot about Vietnam, but she knew he'd had some rough experiences there. *In fact*, she thought, *he never did say a lot about himself or his life.*

General Adlerson was frowning to himself. "I have to go now." He was glancing across the field at a uniformed man who was gesturing to him. "What will you two do?"

Kate looked at Chato, whose face was still impassive. "Maybe we could take a car and look over some of the nearby areas," she suggested.

"All right," the general said. "Take my car, and then we'll be able to get in contact with you via the radio."

"Thank you, General Adlerson." She shook hands with him, and Chato nodded coolly.

Kate watched the general as he moved across the runway with a powerful stride. Then she turned to Chato. "You certainly are quiet this morning. Get up on the wrong side of the bed?"

"No," he said shortly.

"What then?"

He shrugged. "I don't know. I just don't have anything to say. I've run out of good humor, I guess."

She sighed and shifted the strap of her shoulder bag.

She could understand that in a way. The air that morning was heavy, ominous. The sun shone from time to time, but for the most part the sky was obscured by gray clouds. It looked almost as if it were going to rain, or snow, but she knew it was too early in the season for that.

Perhaps it was the waiting that was causing this feeling of foreboding. Waiting for that evening, waiting for the Gilas, waiting for … whose death? Gilas' or humans'?

She shivered, and Chato stepped closer to her and put his arm around her. She leaned her head on his shoulder for a moment, then said, "Let's go. All right?"

He nodded, kissed her briefly on the lips, then led the way back to the general's dark-blue car.

They drove the government car about thirty miles outside the city. The surrounding countryside looked as though it had been ravaged by war.

It was war, Chato thought. *Man versus nature. Humans versus Gilas*.

Crushed cars lay in the dirt alongside the highways. Even though the roads had been closed from Torres to Albuquerque, there had been those motorists who had disregarded the barricades or who had gone driving in some misguided sense of curiosity. And they had paid dearly for their curiosity.

The little villages along the south Rio Grande valley had been razed. Nothing moved in the late-morning haze, except for some army workers clearing away the debris.

What good was that? Chato wondered. There would simply be more of it tonight, and if the humans failed, more the night after that….

He and Kate followed a trail of blood that crept from the highway back to an adobe wall, the only thing standing in the small village.

Chato stopped the car, and they got out and looked around.

"Tonight," Kate said, "they'll be active again, and then we'll stop them. Forever."

Chato squinted at her in the glare of the haze, but said nothing. The surviving victims of the latest Gila attack were huddled together on one side of the solitary adobe wall. Blankets were thrown over their shoulders, and many of them wore no shoes. Chato could hear the sound of wailing, and watched as two old women rocked back and forth with grief.

On the ground, here and there, were various bundles, covered with tarps and sheets and blankets, whatever could be found. Some, much smaller than the others, were obviously children and infants.

The unlucky ones, he thought. Or were they? The live ones had to go on, without their families or homes, and with their terrible memories. Lucky to be alive? Maybe.

"Let's go back," he said. "I'd rather wait there."

She nodded, and they returned to the car.

Once back in Albuquerque, Kate saw a restaurant and suggested they get a bite to eat. As they entered, Chato noticed that it was almost empty, like the streets of the city.

"Afraid," Kate said, following his gaze. "They've all fled."

"I don't blame them," he remarked.

"Don't you think we'll be able to stop them?"

"I don't know, but if *I* lived here, I wouldn't be taking any chances either. I'd leave while I could."

The waitress came and they ordered light meals. Chato couldn't eat much; his stomach was in turmoil. *Nerves*, he told himself with a slight smile. *Nerves about tonight, about the lizards. If we don't stop them, the entire city … But what's to keep the Gilas from moving northward, or west, or east. How do we stop them?*

He remembered one of the letters to the editor in the morning edition of the *Courier.* "Nuke the Gilas," it had suggested. They couldn't do that. It would kill too many people. But it *would* kill the Gilas.

Nuke, nuke, nuke. And we've napalmed the southern part of the state.

He thought he'd left Vietnam years ago, but it didn't look that way anymore.

The reports that had come in over the past few days stated that the entire area where the bombs had been dropped was ravaged. Estimates were that nothing would grow there for years. Most of the wildlife had been killed. Because the vegetation was gone, erosion would begin. *We've killed an entire ecological system,* he thought. *Because of these monsters.*

He wondered about the Gilas, wondered if they thought. They certainly had turned back to Holloman Base for revenge, hadn't they? Maybe they had simply sensed where the bombers had come from. Sure.

What compelled them northward? They had been mutated because of the radiation of that first nuclear bomb in 1945. If nuclear weapons were dropped on them now, what would happen? Would they mutate even more?

Are we the dinosaurs of the present, and are they the thinking creatures of the future?

No opposable thumb, he pointed out to himself. Details, details, details.

"Hey!"

"Hey, what?" His attention returned to the restaurant and to Kate, who was staring at him with an odd expression on her face.

"Hey, I'm here. Remember?"

"Sure. It'd be hard to forget." He tried to leer, but failed.

Her hand covered his. He gave her a small smile, then resumed eating his cold cheeseburger.

The restaurant was quiet. No one spoke; there was no music. A somber lot. The few other customers in the place glanced at the couple from time to time.

Kate must have been recognized, Chato thought. Her picture had been in every newspaper in New Mexico and across the country. Even in foreign countries. He had seen his picture, too, in one of the newsmagazines. "Scientist's Companion," the caption under his picture had read. It hadn't been half bad, except that he'd looked slightly mean. *A mean Indian*, he thought with amusement.

What would happen to Kate at the university? he wondered. *Would they promote her?* Only if they won tonight. Only if they beat the giant menace from the south. Only.

It was so simple.

"Penny for your thoughts?" she teased, glancing up at him.

"They're not worth it."

"Oh, c'mon."

"I was just wondering what you'll do after this is all over." He paused. "It might be sort of dull to go back to teaching a bunch of bubble-brained freshmen."

She shrugged and twisted a red curl around one finger. "I don't know. I haven't given it much thought." But her eyes wouldn't meet his.

"Sure."

"Chato, it's true."

"Okay. I believe you." But he didn't. What did she want out of this? She was using it to further her career. *But what was wrong with that?* he asked himself. *What do you know, Chato, you're just a blanket Indian. Gone back to the reservation, given up your fancy education and the good job with all its promise. Your father is ashamed. Your mother can't understand it. Your brother won't talk to you. You're just a coward.*

You were a good geologist. I still like rocks, told himself, and then almost laughed out loud at the absurdity of it.

"You ready?" he asked.

"Let me pay."

He nodded. He wouldn't argue. After all, she made more money than he did.

She paid and they left, and Chato stared at the deserted streets of the city.

"What do we do until tonight?"

"Wait," she said.

Dusk fell quickly over the city, and they drove south on the highway once more. Kate stopped the car, got out, and looked around.

"They haven't progressed this far yet," she said. She raised her binoculars and surveyed the land. "Look!" She pointed, and Chato peered into the gloom.

Was that some slight movement? He felt a tingle of excitement go through him.

The enemy.

He cocked his head and listened. Very faintly, above the whisper of the slight wind, he could hear a sound. Hissing? He shivered, and strained. It *was* hissing.

"They're coming," he said, and felt a little foolish for saying the obvious.

Kate spoke into the radio. "General Adlerson, this is Dr. Dwyer. Chato and I are ten miles south of the city and we can hear them coming already…. How long? Thirty minutes. No more, I'm sure…. Yes, yes. We'll wait here for ten minutes, then we'll head back toward town…. No, sir, we won't get caught. Yes, thank you, and the same to you, sir."

She joined Chato, who was watching intently toward the south. "The Air Force bombers are taking off now."

The B-52s with the liquid nitrogen canisters in the bomb bays. Fighters out of Kirtland and what was left of the 227th Tactical Fighter Wing out of Holloman.

He thought he could see the glint of the lizards' yellow eyes, but he knew he was imagining things. He had seen them up close that one time, and he didn't much care to be in their proximity again.

"How long until the bombers are here?" he asked.

She glanced at her watch. "Twenty minutes now."

"When do we leave?"

"When the Gilas are getting close."

He looked at Kate, studied her profile. She was watching southward, occasionally looking into the binoculars. What did she want? A stuffed and mounted Gila? Did she imagine herself the great white hunter?

"There!" She pointed, and there was a tremor of excitement in her voice.

Chato followed her finger and saw them. Huge creatures, lined against the darkening sky. Slithering toward them, crawling. He could feel the force of their feet on the ground, and he wondered how many there were. Dozens, hundreds, maybe even thousands. No one had ever counted the creatures, and it wasn't likely they would stop to have a census taken.

He could faintly see the yellow of their eyes now, and he could hear the rise of that awful sound.

Hiss. Hiss. Hiss.

"How many minutes now?" he asked anxiously.

"Fifteen," she replied.

That was all? It felt as though it had been a lifetime since she'd talked to the general.

"What if the liquid nitrogen doesn't work? What if the bombers drop their load and the Gilas live through it? What then, Kate? We don't know how much they've mutated." He glanced at her, saw her lips tighten. "I don't think it'll be much of a worry for us, Chato," she said slowly in a tone that chilled him. "We'll be dead."

He shivered and watched as the giant lizards approached.

Chapter 23

Closer and closer the lizards crawled. Chato felt the hair prickle along his arms and the back of his neck. He began to sweat. "I don't know about you, hon, but I'm not the martyr type. Let's go. Okay?"

"One moment." She sounded distracted, remote. Going over to the car, she opened the trunk and brought something out. There was a rattle of keys as she slammed the trunk down.

Curiosity overcame common sense, and Chato walked over to investigate. "What's that you've got?" He stared. "A camera?"

"Yes. Outfitted for night work."

"Christ, Kate! This is hardly the time to take pictures of these things!"

"On the contrary," she said with a slightly cold tone to her voice, "I can't think of a better time. I wasn't prepared for it last time, but now I am."

"Kate!"

"Don't worry, Chato, I won't risk your neck."

"You already are," he grumbled. "*Our* necks."

"We've gotten through it so far, haven't we?"

"Yeah, but we haven't been standing around waiting for an army of giant Gila monsters to march over us." She calmly patted his hand and walked away. He watched as she snapped photo after photo of the advancing army.

Minutes, precious minutes, seemed to tick away, and his shirt felt clammy on his back.

"Got enough?"

"I'll let you know when I'm finished, Chato."

She was foolish, dumb like all these scientists, he told himself. They all had martyr complexes, that's that it was. They wanted to sacrifice themselves for the sake of science. Well, dammit, he didn't. He had a lot of years ahead and he certainly didn't want to end up as some giant lizard's bedtime snack.

"Kate!" There was more urgency in his voice.

Where were those planes? Had they been delayed? They'd better get the hell out of there, if they didn't want to get bombed with liquid nitrogen as well.

"Come on!" he said.

"Okay," she said triumphantly. "I've got them." She swung the camera's strap over her shoulder. "Let's go, Chato." She paused with her hand on the handle of the car door. "Do you have the keys?"

"No, I thought you did." He glanced south. The lizards were well in sight. He fought the churning in his stomach.

"C'mon, Chato, let's not play games." Her voice was impatient.

"Games?" he asked blankly. "What games?"

"Games. You know."

"No, honey, I don't know what you mean. I don't have the keys." He searched his pockets quickly, thinking she might have tossed them to him and he had forgotten, but he found nothing. He grabbed her purse and dumped the contents onto the back seat of the car. Compact, wallet, house keys, pens. But no car keys.

"Jesus," he said. "Jesus." He went around to the back of the car and ran his hands over the trunk, past the lock, then knelt down and began searching. That rattle … when she opened the trunk; the keys were gone.

"Hurry, Chato," she urged.

"I am."

Nothing but pebbles and some candy wrappers. "No go."

Overhead they could hear the drone of planes. The hissing grew louder.

"What'll we do?" she asked, and for the first time he heard a frantic note in her voice.

He looked up into the sky. Occasionally he could see the lights of the bombers in a break in the clouds. Directly above them he saw moonlight reflected off a Huey helicopter.

In minutes the bombers would be overhead, dropping their liquid nitrogen ... killing the lizards ... killing them, if they didn't get the hell out of there.

"We run," he said, and he grabbed Kate's hand. Behind them the first lizard broke away from the others. The couple sprinted back toward the city, away from the lizards, away from the death-filled bombers. Chato could hear the tread of the monster's feet as it pursued them. *God, don't let us fail,* he prayed silently. Across the anthills and through the cacti they ran, oblivious to anything except the sound of the hissing behind them and the distant rumble of the bombers overhead.

The sound of the planes' engines intensified. Chato paused long enough to take one look over his shoulder. A rain of bombs fell from the night sky drenching the area where they had been standing not more than ten minutes before.

Still pursuing them, though, was the lizard that had missed the deadly liquid nitrogen.

Chato gripped Kate's hand even tighter and pulled her on. She hadn't said a word since they'd begun their flight, and when he glanced at her face, it was white, pinched, frightened.

He could imagine what the lizards would look like now, those that had been caught. *If the stuff had worked*, he told himself.

It would have spread out and drenched the Gilas. And slowly the monsters would have stopped, frozen in their tracks, huge heads raised, straining to look ahead, some clawed feet raised in midpace.

God, what if some of the planes pursued the beast that was chasing them? What if the bomber pilots—and how could they know?—weren't aware that he and Kate were there? After all, they had been expected to leave much earlier.

Good-bye, Chato and Kate, he told himself grimly.

There was a whirring of blades overhead and they both glanced up. There was a dark shape against the silver clouds, and for a moment the moon broke through. Not a grasshopper, as he'd first thought, not a giant one, but rather a helicopter, the Huey he'd seen earlier. He saw something white and sinuous float down. He tugged at Kate's hand and pointed.

A rope ladder.

They raced toward it, and with an almost demonical surge Chato seized Kate, practically flinging her at the rope. She clutched at it with both hands and clambered up the rungs. He started to grab the ladder when the hissing sounded close behind him.

Momentarily the helicopter lifted; the ladder was out of his grasp. He stumbled; then, cursing, he ran, not looking back.

He could hear the lizard behind him, could feel the fetid breath, hear the hissing so close to him … so close … it was going to get him. He prayed to the old gods, gods that he hadn't thought about in a long time.

He was running without thinking, his legs pumping harder than they had ever done before, but the lizard was faster, and it was going to get him, and he could feel the immense flat head reaching toward him. The mouth was opening, wider and wider, and there were the rows of ugly teeth dripping their poisonous venom. The smell of it curdled his stomach and he almost vomited.

Then, ahead, the ladder appeared, and he threw himself at it in one last burst of energy. It had to work, he told himself. It had to, because he had nothing left, nothing. He gripped the rope and hung on. *Let them lift*, he prayed, *let them lift*.

And then the Gila monster was snapping at him, missing his body by inches.

Slowly, so slowly it seemed an eternity, the helicopter lifted, and the creature tried to get him one last time. He saw the yellow eyes below him, and they glinted with an evil light he'd never seen before in a living creature. He shivered, seeing that look, knowing the creature had been determined to kill him.

But now the helicopter was lifting him up and away, away from the jaws of death.

He was free. He hung on to the rope ladder as it swung back and forth, and he stared down at the beast, now frozen in midsnap.

He closed his eyes. It was going to be all right.

Chapter 24

"Got the tickets, Chato?" Kate looked back over her shoulder at him.

"Yeah. They're right here." He waved them at her, then winked. "Thanks again for inviting me. I've always wanted to see the world."

"You should have been a marine," Kate replied with a laugh.

"No, thanks. I've already served my time."

In the three weeks since the last of the giant Gila monsters had been killed, Kate had received numerous offers from universities around the world to lecture on the giant killer lizards. Not wanting to travel alone, she had asked Chato to accompany her. He had thought it over for a full thirty seconds before heartily accepting.

They walked through security and the metal-detecting door, down the long subterranean tunnel, and then up the escalator to the satellite terminal at the Albuquerque International Airport.

International, Kate thought with amusement. With international flights only to Mexico. Well, perhaps someday they would have direct flights to Europe. Someday, but not now.

"We're in luck," Chato said, staring out one of the windows of the satellite. "The plane's already here."

"Umm?" She was rummaging through her new handbag. She'd had to replace quite a lot, as her old purse and wallet had been left behind in the government car when that last Gila had chased them.

When they had returned to the site the following day, only a crushed shell of the car had remained.

Chato had remarked that it looked as if the entire army of Gilas had deliberately walked over the car, and perhaps he was right; perhaps they had known, after all, whom they had been fighting.

Luckily, she thought, wryly, the State Vehicle Department had been wonderfully cooperative about replacing her driver's license, and the credit companies had been quick about new cards.

That day ... she remembered it with a shiver. And Chato had been proven correct in his vision of the dead Gila monsters.

Hundreds of giant lizard corpses were strewn from the southern outskirts of Albuquerque to the tiny town of Bosque Farms, some thirty miles away. They were all turned north, all of them, almost single-minded in their direction.

It was uncanny, she'd thought as they walked through the miles of dead Gilas, miles that stretched to the banks of the Rio Grande. No one had spoken: not Kate, not Chato, not General Adlerson, not the Air Force specialists who had come out there with them.

Walking among them, Kate thought it was difficult to believe the creatures had ever been alive. They looked like statues, something out of an amusement park, and Chato had remarked in an undertone that the state government would probably close off the area and declare it a state park. She had thought he was joking, until she looked up and saw his eyes.

Even by that morning of the inspection the pools of venom had not yet dried up, and they had carefully skirted the soggy areas filled with the foul liquid.

Even when the press had been allowed in at last to take pictures, there had been a subdued air. There had been none of the casual bantering she knew was so common among the press people. Nothing but silence. It was as though the sight of these huge mute monsters, these terrible creatures that had wrought so much damage in so little time, had wiped away any words the journalists might have spoken.

The reports in the newspapers had been accurate, but not sensational. Subdued, again.

But now two of the national television networks wanted to do specials on the Gilas, and she was to have a featured spot in each one. The third network, not to be outdone, was planning a weekly TV drama series, the first episode to feature the Gilas.

What next? she'd wondered when Chato had told her of that. He had suggested perhaps a heartwarming tale of a Gila-monster family, but she hadn't smiled at his half-jest.

Her face and Chato's were splashed on every front page of every major, and not so major, newspaper and magazine across the country and around the world. She'd had hundreds of phone calls every day from curiosity-seekers, journalists, souvenir-hunters. She'd finally had to change to an unlisted phone number, and then, when the people kept coming to the door of her apartment and ringing the bell, even at three A.M., she and Chato had relocated to a motel.

It wasn't the Golden Palomino Motel, but it would do, she thought, and laughed silently.

And the university, impressed with her part in destroying the Gila-monster menace, had rewarded her. Not only was she Dr. Dwyer; she was now Professor. A full professorship. And that meant more money, more prestige, more freedom to do what she wanted to do. She was now a Big Name at the university.

Everyone wanted her to write a book about her experiences. There was even a contract from a studio in Hollywood about a movie, but she hadn't gotten to talk to the man because Chato had chased him away.

Dear Chato, Kate thought, looking at his profile, now that they were seated comfortably in the plane. How was he handling it, this instant fame? He seemed to be the same as always, the same. It hadn't turned his head at all. He was, after all, the same ol' Chato.

But had it turned hers? she wondered. Maybe ... a little, she conceded. It was hard not to be influenced. It *had* been her plan, after all, that had led to the destruction of the monstrous reptiles. Hers and hers alone.

And for that, both she and Chato had received citations of merit from the new governor; they had been flown to the White House to dine with the President and First Lady, and there was the promise of meeting foreign heads of state, once they were overseas.

Not bad, not bad at all, Kate Dwyer, she told herself. Far better than dissecting snakes and getting formaldehyde all over your pants.

Now, there would be the tour. She braced herself as the plane hurtled down the mile-long runway, then took off, her least favorite time of flight. When she opened her eyes again, all she could see outside was the blue of the sky, tinged with fleecy clouds.

Twenty countries, twenty-eight cities, four months. She thought they would have enough time to see a few things, travel around a bit, and sample the food as well as the culture.

"Travel is broadening," she murmured.

"Hmm?" Chato looked up from the paperback novel he was reading. "What'd you say?"

"I said, travel is broadening."

"I know." He winked at her and returned to his book. She glanced at the title. A political book. She didn't recognize the name. Something-or-other Foster. She shrugged and closed her eyes.

Here it was mid-October. Autumn was a fine time to travel, especially in Europe. After that, during the winter, they were to go to the Far East on tour.

Three weeks ago ... and three weeks of mopping up in New Mexico. It would be a long time, she thought, before the state recovered.

And in that time, among all the citations and accolades, she'd had time to examine some of the Gila corpses. But the really great thing about being famous was that she didn't have to do all the hard, dirty work, such as cutting up the creatures, though in the end she got all the credit.

She had jokingly asked Chato if he'd like to help by dissecting one of the giant lizards with a blowtorch. To her surprise, he had quickly shaken his head and backed off, muttering something about lizards being bad spirits to Apaches.

God, those three weeks had been full. So much had happened; so much left to do; she could hardly believe it was October.

Autumn. Kate frowned momentarily, as something whispered in her mind. Opening her eyes, she looked around at the interior of the plane.

Something was wrong; something was bothering her. Nagging at her subconscious. Something very important.

She stared at Chato's profile, but he was deeply engrossed in reading and didn't turn. Something. Something.

In her mind she reviewed the hundreds of pages of reports that her assistants had filed. She flipped the pages over mentally and scanned them once more.

Autumn.

Three weeks ago, and then ten days before that … early September.

And there it was, that crucial paragraph, in some report that she had glanced at, but hadn't yet studied. So important.

"Oh, my God," she said out loud.

"What?" Chato looked up.

"Oh, my God," she repeated.

"What is it, Kate?" His black eyes were filled with concern, and he placed one of his hands on hers. He set the paperback down in his lap.

171

"We've got to contact the governor at once." She struggled out of her seat belt, then stood. One of the flight attendants began swaying down the aisle toward her.

"What is it, Kate?" Chato repeated.

"The state is going to be threatened by more lizards," she said, her voice becoming slightly shrill. Some of the passengers looked up at her.

"Kate, that's impossible. The Gilas have all been destroyed. Destroyed before they could lay their eggs. You know that." He smiled reassuringly at her, and she knew what he was thinking, that she was suffering some sort of hallucination, that she was experiencing nightmares from the hellish night. Both had, for weeks after, and they would wake sweat-drenched and hold each other until they drifted off to an uneasy slumber once more. But this was different. This was *real*.

"No, Chato. No." The flight attendant now stood beside her, and had put his hand on her arm.

"May I help you, Dr. Dwyer?" the young man asked.

She seemed to ignore him and turned eyes filled with dread to Chato, who was still seated. "Those weren't the adults we killed, Chato." She watched as the color drained from his face. "Not the adults. A report by one of my assistants said that these specimens were not fully matured.

"Don't you realize what this means? These were just the newly hatched babies. September would have been at the end of their incubation period, and they must have hatched sometime in early September. Babies, just babies. Do you understand?"

Tears streamed down her face, and she stared at him.

Chato could find nothing to say. He simply looked out the airplane window, down below at the state of New Mexico, which had thought the nightmare was over.

Instead, it was just about to begin.

Just outside Albuquerque, the ground seemed to shake and heave, to roll and pull apart, as though from an earthquake. Sands shifted, and Gila monsters, a hundred feet in length, their evil yellow eyes glinting in the autumn moonlight, crawled into the unsuspecting city.

About the Author

Kathryn Ptacek sold her first novel, SATAN'S ANGEL, when she was just 27. Since then she has sold numerous novels, short stories, reviews, articles, and miscellaneous whatnots. She has also edited three anthologies, including the landmark WOMEN OF DARKNESS and WOMEN OF DARKNESS II.

Kathy was raised in Albuquerque, New Mexico, and graduated with a degree in journalism from the University of New Mexico. While there, she was a student of bestselling authors Tony Hillerman (mysteries) and Lois Duncan (young adult). She also has a freelance editing business, Little Bird Editorial Services.

She lives in a 140-year-old Victorian house haunted by the ghost of her late husband, writer Charles L. Grant. She shares her book-cluttered rooms with four cats, a large teapot collection, lots of Gila monster stuff, and the occasional visiting mouse. Kathy can be reached at gilaqueen@att.net or through her Facebook pages.

Book List

Horror and Suspense Novels
And No Birds Sing
Blood Autumn
Ghost Dance
Gila!
In Silence Sealed
Kachina
Looking Backwards in Darkness
Shadoweyes
The Hunted

Fantasy Novels written as Kathryn Grant
The Land of a Thousand Willows Trilogy
The Phoenix Bells
The Black Jade Road
The Willow Garden

Historical Novels written as Kathryn Atwood
Satan's Angel
Renegade Lady
The Lawless Heart
My Lady Rogue
Aurora

Historical Romance Novels written as Kathleen Maxwell
The Devil's Heart
Winter Masquerade

Curious about other Crossroad Press books? Stop by our
website: http://crossroadpress.com
We offer quality writing
in digital, audio, and print formats.

Subscribe to our newsletter on the website homepage and receive
a free eBook.